Really-Truly Stories

Really-Truly Stories

Volume

5

Gwendolyn Lampshire Hayden

Pacific Press®
Publishing Association

Nampa, Idaho | Oshawa, Ontario, Canada
www.pacificpress.com

Illustrated by Vernon Nye

Revised ed. Copyright © 1983 by Pacific Press® Publishing Association
Printed in the United States of America

The author assumes full responsibility for the accuracy of all facts
and quotations as cited in this book.

You can obtain additional copies of this book by calling toll-free
1-800-765-6955 or by visiting http://www.adventistbookcenter.com.

ISBN 978-0-8163-6290-5

February 2017

Contents

1

Mines, Misers, and America

JOEL clutched his carefully wrapped lunch and hurried by the silent schoolhouse that stood empty and forlorn in the cold morning light.

"Six-forty!" he thought sleepily. "And I've *got* to be at work by seven o'clock. It'll never do for me to be late. I'll just have to make a run for Shepherd's Mine and trust to luck and my two good legs to get me there on time.

"But tomorrow morning I certainly won't turn over in bed for those last forty winks of sleep. That extra cat nap's what made me get a late start today."

Joel's feet broke into a quick dogtrot that carried him past the village houses and down the winding lane that led to the large lead mine near Goonhavern. As he jogged along, his thoughts flew wistfully back to the school he had just passed and from which he had some months ago been promoted.

"Well, at least I've completed the sixth standard" [the top grammar school grade in England], he thought wistfully, "and that's as far as anyone can go in this school. I'd give a pretty penny to be able to get away to some larger place where I could go on with my studies. But what's the use of wishing such a thing! Mother can't afford to send me anywhere. And now that I'm fifteen past I should be helping her."

Joel's busy thoughts seemed to keep step with his hurrying feet, so that by the time he reached the mine entrance he was quite out of breath.

"Well, I wondered when you'd get here! I'd say you slept too long," laughed red-cheeked Arthur. He was the largest of the four other lads who worked from seven A.M. to five P.M. under the eagle-eyed supervision of a mine foreman.

"You're right," nodded Joel. He looked around quickly for their foreman, who, exactly on the stroke of seven, began to break up the larger rocks streaked with ore and pass them on to the boys. Joel's arms ached as he thought of another day of back-breaking labor over the ore that must be hammered down to the size of cabbages before being sent on to the smelter.

"There's Tom Simmons now," whispered Arthur. "He's getting ready to start up the skip. That means we'll soon be swinging our sledge hammers."

Joel glanced toward the mine shaft, whose ladder ran straight down hundreds of feet into the earth's dark interior. He watched as the sturdy miners emerged, one by one, from the boiler room, clad in their tannish-colored, two-piece garments and their hard hats that protected them from falling rocks. He felt pity for them as they began their long descent into the mine. Half-fearfully, he watched as they started carefully down the ladder, rung by rung.

Well he knew how they would look when they pulled themselves wearily toward the daylight after long hours of work in the dark underground tunnels. He could picture them, soaked to the skin from the water that constantly seeped into the mine, with their burned-out miner's candles still stuck in the daubs of clay they had plastered on their foreheads as candle holders.

Thud! Thud! Thud! rang Joel's hammer on the hard ore. Thud! Thud! Thud! "And this is the way you earn sixpence [twelve cents] a day." The echoes seemed to ring in his ears as he worked steadily, with only a short noon hour in which to eat the crusty meat-and-potato pasty that seemed all too small to satisfy his boyish hunger.

He was thankful when the five o'clock quitting signal was given and the skip, with its last load of ore, was stopped above ground.

"Another day's over," he said to Arthur. "And am I glad! I'd give a lot to be doing anything else but working in this lead mine in Cornwall, England, right now."

"What'd you like to do?" inquired the practical Arthur. "Mining's about the only work around here. At least it's all my family knows. How else could you earn a living, Joel?"

"Oh, I don't know," Joel answered soberly. "If I was really lucky, maybe I could get a job like the one my brother John has now. He just finished sixth standard too, but he went over to Callington and got employment with a grocer. He gets all of a half crown [sixty cents] a week and room and board besides. And, in addition, he's learning the trade.

"Maybe someday he'll get a chance to go to America and have a store of his own. If so, I'll get to go out there and help him."

"A store of his own!" echoed Arthur scornfully. "You must be dreaming. How would he ever get enough money to go all the way across the ocean to America to set up shop there? Why, folks say your father's been in America for years, and he's never even made enough to send for one of your family yet. If he can't earn enough money as a grown man, how do you think you and John could get over there and start up your own business?"

Joel felt his cheeks burn as Arthur talked. He swallowed hard to keep back the angry words that almost tumbled out, for well he knew that his companion but echoed the opinion of the villagers.

"I won't say anything," he thought grimly. "I won't. He just doesn't understand that someday Father really *will* have good luck in America. He can't understand that someday he'll find a nice place for us and make enough money to pay our passage over there.

"And when that day comes and I'm ready to leave, I'd like to walk right up to Arthur. I'd like to be able to say, 'All right, Arthur, how about it? Am I going to America or am I staying here to work with you in Shepherd's Mine? Answer me, now.' I guess he'll have to eat his words then, whether he likes their taste or not!"

"Well," concluded Arthur, "it looks as if we'd all be looking for other work, whether we want to or not.

I overheard Tim telling some of the men that the mine was shutting down next week."

"Shutting down! Shutting down next week!" All the way home the dismal words echoed in Joel's ears. All the way home his feet lagged, for he dreaded the thought of telling his mother.

"Never mind, son," soothed Mother, as he stammered out the unwelcome news of the mine's closing. "From something your brother John said to me the last time he was home on a visit, I think you can get work over in St. Agnes. He told me that if the mine should close down you could come to him for a short time. Then he'd find employment for you with a grocer he knows in a nearby village.

"He said you'd get room and board as a grocer's apprentice but no money for a while. However, you'd be learning the grocery trade as a means of earning your livelihood later on. Such training would be invaluable to you, Joel, for you well know that I can't afford to send you away for further schooling. I'd hoped and prayed that long before now your father would have been able to send for us to come to America. But years have gone by since he sailed from England. And still he's been able to send us only a few checks."

"But, Mother," he interrupted hastily, "don't you think Father'll really begin making money in the Nevada mines? Now that he's well again, and Uncle Bill's over his long sickness, he'll surely be able to save something for us. Bad luck can't last forever!"

"I hope not, son, I hope not," sighed Mother. Joel's heart ached as he saw her work-worn hands wipe away

the tears that dropped slowly down upon her starched apron.

"Never mind, Mother," he said fiercely. "We may be poor now, but someday we'll all be together in America. And when we get there I'm going on to school. And then I'm going to get a good job, so that you'll never have to work again. When we get to America, we're going to have so much to eat that we'll *never* be hungry."

"Now, now, Joel," laughed Mother shakily. She smiled lovingly through her tears at her blue-eyed, black-haired boy. "It's true we've had some hard times; but still we've never starved, and I don't think we ever will. I've always said I'd never let my children go hungry as long as I could be trusted for a sack of flour at Mrs. Martin's store. And I never have."

"W-ell, that's true," nodded Joel. "But we've come pretty close to it a good many times—too close for comfort. And it isn't fair for you to have to work so hard all the time, Mother. I don't like it.

"Oh, I wish Father could find some place for us in America. If we could only get over there, I just know we'd get along all right. I just *know* we would."

All during the following weeks and months Joel kept repeating this belief to himself, even on days that were so dark and dismal he almost despaired of a brighter future. He doggedly recalled his determination to work hard and do well in his apprenticeship with the fat grocer whose sharp black eyes had stared so hard at him as John introduced them.

"So this is the lad, eh?" Mr. Beadle had grunted on that distant day.

"Yes, sir," replied Joel politely.

"Hm-m. Fifteen going on sixteen, you say?"

"That's correct," answered John. "And I'm sure, Mr. Beadle, that you'll find him a good worker, too, no matter what you ask him to do."

"So? H-mm! That we'll soon see. Looks spindling to do much heavy lifting. Not very big for his age."

"Oh, I'm strong enough, sir," quickly answered Joel. "You see, sir, I've been working in a mine since I finished the sixth standard.

"At the mine I helped pick over the lead ore as it was hoisted up on the skip. Then I'd break up the larger chunks. Oh, I'm strong enough for any work here, I'm sure, Mr. Beadle."

"You're nothing but a sissy—a sissy—a sissy. You couldn't lift a cup of treacle with both hands," interrupted a hateful, whining voice. Joel and John turned quickly and just in time to see the young newcomer stick out a very red tongue at them.

"Now, now, Cyril," said Mr. Beadle fondly. "Do be a good boy and run along. This here is no business of yours at all. It——"

" 'Tis so," rudely interrupted young Master Beadle. "I don't like that boy's looks," he said, pointing a sticky, candy-streaked forefinger at Joel. "I don't want him here. He hadn't better stay, either. If he does, I'll be so mean to him he'll pack up and leave just like your last apprentice did."

"Cyril!" shrilled a high voice from somewhere upstairs. "Cy-ril. Come here, darling. I need you. Come along right now. That's a good boy."

"Well," said Mr. Beadle briskly, as Cyril slowly departed, red tongue still pointed in their direction, " 'boys will be boys' they do say. And now might we call our little business finished? I've just lost my apprentice, and I need one badly, what with new goods coming to the store tomorrow to be unpacked and all.

"Shall we say you're to start now, Joel? Here you can learn the grocery trade and have your room and board while you're learning. I might say you'll be almost like one of the family. Bring your bag with me. I'll show you where you're to sleep."

"Like one of the family!" thought Joel bitterly, months later. "Up early and late to bed. And always, always, pestered by that horrid Cyril. I'd have gone home long ago if I could have gotten any work there. But I can't go home and be a burden on Mother.

"No, I'll just have to stay and do the best I can, though I can't do much with this sore hand. It's getting worse instead of better. Looks as if it's swelling up more all the time. Whew! it even hurts when I cut kindling to start the morning fire. And I've got to hurry, or Mrs. Beadle'll be here before it's laid and burning."

"Ouch! Don't bump against my arm, Cyril," said Joel sharply. "My left hand hurts. It's been sore ever since you scratched me the other day."

"I should've scratched your other hand, too," snarled Cyril. He danced from one foot to the other like a grinning jumping jack. "And I'll bump your hand if I want to. Besides, you're cutting kindling with Papa's knife, ain't you?"

"No, I'm not," flared Joel. "I'm using my own knife.

Now run along and leave me alone. You shouldn't be up so early anyway. I've got work to do as soon as I get this fire started!"

"Papa!" screamed the untruthful Cyril. "Joel's cutting kindling with your knife. He is so! Joel's cutting kindling with your go-oo-d knife."

"Stop it!" commanded Joel. As the older boy dropped the knife and reached for the young troublemaker, he saw Cyril strike hard at his outstretched, swollen hand.

Slap!

"OW!" cried Joel. He stopped still and glared angrily at the grinning child. "Don't you dare tell such lies. And don't you dare hit me like that."

"I will if I want to," mocked Cyril. "You're nothing but my father's 'prentice. And I'll hit you if I want to. So there!"

Slap!

Again Cyril aimed at Joel's swollen hand.

Crack! Joel struck out in self-defense.

"OW-w-w-w!" screamed Cyril. As his hand flew to his reddened cheek, he burst into tears. "Y-you hit me! Papa never hits me!" he wailed.

"Too bad for you that Papa never does," muttered Joel, nursing his own throbbing fingers. "You'd be a better boy if you got a few whacks once in a while." He recalled his own mother's belief in "Spare the rod and spoil the child."

Running footsteps told the boys of the rapid approach of Cyril's ever-doting father.

"Here! Here! What's all this?" wheezed nightgown-clad Mr. Beadle. "What's going on here? Why, there's positively so much noise a man can't decently rest."

"Joel's been cutting kindling with your knife, Papa," sniffed Cyril, "and he slapped me, too."

"What?" roared Mr. Beadle, now thoroughly awake. "You struck my son? How dare you slap my child, you impertinent upstart!"

"Then make him stop lying about me, Mr. Beadle," replied Joel firmly but courteously. "I haven't been using your knife to cut kindling. And I didn't intend to slap Cyril, even though he was untruthful. But he hit my sore hand. And before I knew what I was doing I hit him."

Long afterward Joel could smile about that early morning scene in the kitchen. But that hour and the days that followed before his discharge were the dreariest that he was ever to know. Although he sensed that Mr. Beadle believed in his truthfulness, he also knew that no one could criticize young Master Cyril, who was the idol of the senior Beadle's heart. And he was not surprised when Mr. Beadle spoke to him, told him that his mother had sent for him, and that he need not return to work.

"You've been here almost a year now," said Mr. Beadle in closing. "That's much longer than I've kept an apprentice before."

"Or ever will again, as long as Cyril's here," Joel longed to say. But he dared not speak, lest his employer refuse to recommend him to another position.

"Now, you've been a good worker. That I'll say," continued grocer Beadle, grudgingly. "But you're a trifle too hot-headed to get along with Cyril. 'Boys will be boys,' you know, and he's full of little pranks, though he don't mean no harm to anyone.

"So, all considered, I think it best that I get someone else. I'll give you a letter so you can find another place. And I hope you'll learn to hold your temper better than you have here."

Joel watched Mr. Beadle's fat jaws quiver as the grocer shook his head and walked with Joel out to the waiting wagon.

"Harry's going all the way to Goonhavern, so you'll have a ride home," he said in farewell. "Now be a proper and respectful lad. Mind your manners, and work hard, and you'll make a living wherever you go."

"But I've not got overly fat on the wages you've paid, Mr. Beadle," thought Joel resentfully, as the horse-drawn wagon moved slowly down the muddy lane, and the fat grocer disappeared forever from Joel's sight.

"No, sir. I'll not get very fat on that dish of twenty tarts, either. Why, you've brought only two pitchers of treacle and two pitchers of scalded cream to pour over them. Quick, Cyril, get more food. I'm still hungry. Bring several beds too. I'm hungry and I'm sleep——"

"Here! Here! Wake up." As from a great distance, Joel heard Harry's hoarse voice and felt the driver's rough hands shaking his shoulders.

"Wake up, I say. You're home. And here's your mother. She's asking whether you're tired and hungry. Stop your dreaming and wake up!"

"Mother!" exclaimed Joel. He opened his sleepy eyes in joyful amazement. "Why, I'm home again. I'm home in Goonhavern.

"Oh, but it's wonderful to see you once more after all these months, Mother. I was just dreaming I was hungry and tired. And then I woke up and found I was home at last. M-m-m! Something smells good. I know what it is, too. Suet and cabbage dumplings and fresh-baked currant cakes!" He all but forgot his injured hand in his excitement.

"You're right, son," smiled Mother. "You're just in time to sit down and eat with us."

"Us?" questioned Joel, now wide awake. "Who's here?"

"John came home today, dear. He's gone on an errand, but he'll be back right away," replied Mother. "I sent for both of you to come as soon as possible after I received the letter."

"The—the letter? A letter from Father?" Joel asked through lips that suddenly felt stiff and numb. "Did—did *the* letter come at last?" Joel felt his cheeks burn with excitement. He heard his mother's kind voice but faintly through the sudden roaring in his ears.

"Indeed, and it *is* the long-awaited letter. But come. Come inside and I'll put it in your own hands that you can read it for yourself. There. What do you think of the news?"

Joel felt his fingers turn all awkward thumbs as he reached for the travel-stained envelope and eagerly pulled out the rustling letter paper. Quickly his eyes scanned the pages.

"A big ranch in the Harney Valley . . . our own house on it . . . regular stagecoach service in here . . . a fine growing community . . . sold enough cattle for

Joel's fare . . . you and John come next . . . good fortune at last, dear ones. . . ."

Joel heard his voice skimming rapidly through the breath-taking news. "Oh, it's too good to be true. At last we're going to America!" he exclaimed before he handed the letter to his mother. "Within the next year the three of us will join Father in Oregon."

He saw that his mother's long pent-up tears had brimmed over and splashed upon the envelope's penciled address. Somehow, without any words being spoken, in his boyish way he understood how her heart was torn with joy and pain. There was joy that he and John could have new opportunities in America; joy that their little family would once again be united; pain at the thought of the loved friends who would be left behind. He listened as his mother turned toward his brother, who had just entered the doorway.

"Yes, dear ones," she said, "our time of anxious waiting is almost over. With God's help and blessing, we'll soon be on the way to our new home."

"It's half a world away, Mother." Joel thought that John's voice sounded very deep and very sober.

"That's true," she replied. "But—America! I can scarcely realize what this will mean to us." Joel saw his brave little mother wipe away her glistening teardrops before she smiled at each of them.

"Come into the kitchen, boys, and we'll eat. Then after I see what can be done for that sore hand of yours, Joel, we'll talk over our plans. There's work aplenty to be outlined if we get you ready for a January sailing date."

"America! Get ready! January sailing date———" The words rolled through Joel's head until he felt fairly dizzy with excitement. In his mind's eye he saw a series of pictures: the steamer waiting at the Liverpool wharf; the huge, sprawling city of New York; a long, winding train puffing across the width of North America; the stagecoach journey onward from the railroad's end———

"Perhaps there'll even be Indians there," he said aloud, staring into space.

"Indians? Where? Oh, you mean in America," answered John, smilingly. "Well, there may be, but I don't think they'll hurt you."

"I'm not afraid of Indians anyway," firmly replied Joel. "After working first in a lead mine and then for that miserly Beadle family, I don't think I'll ever be afraid of anything again. Not even wild Indians could be worse than Cyril Beadle.

"But first there's one thing I'm going to do," he concluded. "As soon as we finish eating I'm going to run and find Arthur. When we worked together in Shepherd's Mine, I told him the day would come when Father'd send the money for my passage to America.

"Now that day has come. I can hardly wait to see Art's expression when I tell him the good news. And I only wish I could see Cyril's candy-coated face when he learns that I'm really going to sail.

"After all these years I'm going across the ocean to join Father. Surely the coming months will be exciting ones for all of us."

2

From Cornwall to Cattle Country

"OUCH! OW! That hurts, Mother." Joel gritted his teeth as his mother and John bent over his swollen hand and pressed gently along the back of his reddened fingers.

"Where does it pain most of all?" questioned Mother. She looked anxiously at the shiny, tight-stretched skin and the stiffened fingers.

"There. Ouch! Right there. No. All over, I guess. Oh, I can't tell," groaned Joel. "My whole arm aches. It's been like this for days. Mrs. Beadle tried two or three kinds of poultices on it, but none of them did any good. It hurts so bad I can hardly rest at night. That's why I went sound asleep in the wagon on the way home."

"Do you know what I'm going to do?" Mother replied briskly. "I'm going to try a remedy that our old neighbor next door told me about not long ago. When one of her grandchildren had a sore foot she made a poultice that really proved to be a cure-all.

"She heated up some bramble leaves in a pan on the stove. When the blackberry leaves got all dry and crisp she pounded them into small bits and mixed them with lime. Then she put this mixture on the inflamed place, and it drew out all the soreness and swelling.

"I think this treatment will heal your hand, son. At any rate, we'll try it, for something must be done at once or you're likely to have a bad case of blood poisoning."

Joel watched in dread as the mixture was heated and prepared. But a long sigh of relief burst from his lips as the hot poultice clung to his tortured hand.

"That really feels good, Mother," he said. "I think it is going to help. I believe my hand'll get well in time for me to sail in January."

And help it did, Joel reflected happily, as he stood on deck and stared from his recently healed hand to the hurrying crowds that surged about him. He almost trembled from the excitement of his first journey by train from the little town of Truro to the huge, sprawling city of Liverpool, with its crowded wharf.

"I can't believe that I'm really on board ship, waiting to sail out of the harbor, away from England and toward America. England is my homeland, and I love it. But, oh, I'm fortunate to be going to a country where everyone has an opportunity to take up the work he likes best. I'm fortunate to be going where I can earn more than twelve cents a day for my hard work.

"I'm going to do the best I can wherever I am or whatever I'm doing. Maybe I'll even have a chance to go on to school for a while. I want to learn all l can about *everything*."

Joel jumped as the steamer's hoarse blast shook the foggy air. He stared wildly about as he thought that at

last the big ship might be sailing after two days' wait in the fogbound Mersey River. He shivered with a cold chill as the engines' sudden throbbing sent a quiver through the decks.

"Looks as though we're off," cried a cheery voice close behind him. "Guess we're really sailing at last. How do you feel? Sort of shaky in the stomach? I do."

"Shaky is the right word," laughed Joel. He smiled at the rosy-cheeked lad who had spoken to him. "Right now I'm so excited I don't know whether I'm coming or going. But—say! Feel that motion? We're moving, sure and certain."

"About time, too," nodded his curly-headed companion. "The constant noise from those fog horns has been awfully monotonous. They've been sounding day and night since we came on board. Too bad the fog's so thick we can't see anything. I'd counted most awfully on taking in all the sights, especially since I've never before been half this far from St. Ives."

"St. Ives?" exclaimed Joel. "Is that your home? Why, we've almost been neighbors. I've lived most of my life at Goonhavern. Now I'm on my way to my father in Oregon. For a long time he's been working as a miner in the United States. Now he owns a large ranch in eastern Oregon.

"If he's changed a great deal, perhaps I won't know him when we meet. Perhaps my brother John won't know him either. I was only a small boy when father left home, and John is just two years older than I am."

"Say, I guess that'll be some experience," exclaimed his new-found friend. "Are you going to meet your

brother in New York? I hope so, for I don't know anyone there, and I have to go on to a place called Detroit,
Michigan, where my cousins live. I've been wondering
how I'd find my way around in that big city. Folks who've
been there say it's huge."

"Well, we'll get lost together, then," laughed Joel,
"because no one's going to meet me until I get way
out to a place called Burns, in Harney County, eastern
Oregon. My brother won't sail from here until July.
First he'll go to Nevada. Then Mother plans to leave in
August. We can't afford to travel together."

"Oregon!" exclaimed Joel's new traveling companion.
"You *do* have a long way to go. Well, I'm glad I
spoke to you, for at least we can be together halfway
across the United States. I guess we'd better introduce
ourselves."

"I'm certainly glad to meet you, Harry," exclaimed
Joel, as they shook hands. "And I'm glad we're going to
be friends. To tell the truth, I was wondering just how
I *would* get along traveling alone.

"When I came on board ship I was told I'd have
to buy my own mattress if I wanted a place to sleep.
For a while I was afraid I'd have to pay for my meals
too. I don't have any extra money, and I couldn't go in
debt to anyone. Mother'd never allow that!

"I was just about ready to jump overboard and swim
for shore. I thought nine days without food would be a
long, long time."

"You mean eleven days, don't you?" laughed Harry.
"Don't forget we've been here two days already, and
it'll take nine days more to make the Atlantic crossing.

Nine and two make eleven, or else I don't know my numbers.

"Wasn't it a relief to find out we could eat all we wanted and that the price of meals was included in our steamship ticket? I was just like you too, half afraid to ask questions and scared I'd make a mistake."

"Well," replied Joel, "that's why I'm so glad we're together. We may make lots of mistakes from now on, but at least we can make them together, and that'll be some comfort."

Before Harry left the train at Detroit, Joel and Harry had many a good laugh at customs in America. Joel recalled the story his mother's cousin had told of seeing corn on the cob served at an American hotel.

"What in the world are they eating?" he had asked a companion who shared a table with him. He had never seen corn prepared in any other way than cut off and served in small dishes.

His companion was amused. "Oh, you mean that bearded man with those yellow kernels all over his mustache? Why that's corn. Corn on the cob, you know."

Joel chuckled anew as he told how astonished his mother's relative had been. He continued,

"Talking of strange food reminds me of tomatoes. I remember what they look like. One of our neighbors brought several back home to England when he returned from a trip to America. Mother said he must have picked them when they were green, or they'd have spoiled on the way. Anyhow, they didn't look good to me. I don't see how anyone can eat them."

"Nothing looks too good right now," sighed Harry. "I miss my mother's English cooking: meat-and-potato pasties, suet dumplings———"

"Seedy cakes and plum pudding for Christmas and New Year," sighed Joel. All at once he felt homesick for the little village of Goonhavern, which nestled quietly almost within earshot of the waves that dashed against the high, rocky cliffs of Land's End. All at once he felt half a lifetime removed from all that he had known—a stranger in the wide expanse of America.

"Say," began Harry. He cleared his throat and changed the subject almost as though he saw the tell-tale moisture in Joel's blue eyes. "I've got an idea. Why don't we try to find a plum pudding to buy? There surely must be some place in New York where we can buy a tinned one. After all, they're shipped to Australia and India and other places, aren't they?

"If we can get one, we'll at least have something good and filling to eat on the train. Here, I'll ask this police officer. He should be able to help us."

Joel and Harry could scarcely wait for supper hour to arrive on the train. Joel had almost dropped his valise as he ran for the waiting cars, but although he stumbled, he clung fast to the just-purchased plum pudding.

"I wonder if it'll taste at all like Mother's," he said longingly. As Harry finished opening the tin he stared down at the dark, fruity mass within. "Hm-m-m—it's filling, even if that's about all I can truthfully say for it," he added, swallowing hard on a tasteless bite.

"If it's filling, it'll be well worth the purchase price," Harry added. He repeated his statement more than once before he said good-by and left the train in Detroit. "I'll leave you my share of the remaining pudding," he said smilingly, giving Joel a firm handshake.

"Looks as if you'll need it before you get to Burns. You'll have to make that pudding and your money stretch like rubber or you'll be hungry when you get there," he warned. "I wish I had a few extra coins to spare, but I don't. Anyway, you'll make out. It'll be only a few more days now, and then you'll be with your father.

"Good-by and good luck. Even though we may never meet again, I'll often think of you and hope you're able to do all the things you want so very much to do."

"Good-by, Harry. Good-by and good luck to you too," Joel called. He waved a last farewell to his new friend. Then, settling back in his seat, he felt more alone than he had at any time since he first left Goonhavern and had waved good-by to Mother and John.

Clickety-clack. Clickety-clack. Clickety-clack.

Joel woke and slept and woke again. He ate sparingly and drank much water, for he found that water was at least temporarily filling. For hours at a time he stared wonderingly at the broad expanse that was America: the rolling, snow-covered farmlands of Michigan and northern Illinois; the flat, fertile corn country of Iowa and Nebraska; the winter-bleak, arid expanses of Wyoming; the picturesque mountain passes of western Idaho; and then—then the high, desert-like plateau of eastern Oregon.

He caught his breath as the long train ground to a midday stop, and he heard the conductor call, "On-tar-io. Ontario, folks. Step right this way."

He stumbled as he hurried down the aisle, for he felt stiff and lame from days and nights of much sitting and cramped sleeping in his chair-car seat. The crisp, cold wintry air stung in his nostrils and tingled against his hot cheeks as he swung down the steep train steps.

"Mm-m! That feels good," he said under his breath. He looked around quickly for other passengers on the westbound stagecoach and saw five or six people hurrying into the station and the welcome warmth of its glowing coal stove.

"Guess I'd better get in there myself while I'm nice and warm," Joel thought. "There's no sense in standing out in zero weather and getting chilled to the bone. We'll have a long ride today, according to Father's letter. Let's see, now. Just what did he write about the stage schedule?"

Joel pulled off his heavy gloves and reached into his coat pocket for the carefully treasured letter from his father.

"Here it is. We leave Ontario early afternoon and stay at Vale, Oregon, tonight. Tomorrow we'll leave Vale early and stop all night at Beulah. The third night we'll sleep at Pine Creek. And the fourth night we'll be in Burns!

"I wonder what it'll be like in Harney Valley?" All the long journey to his new home, the words kept ringing in Joel's ears. All day as the stagecoach jerked and bounced along over the snowy, rutted roads he tried to picture Father and the new home to which he was going. All night long he dreamed strange dreams in which their well-filled stagecoach lurched along behind the driver's four heavy horses. All night he seemed to hear the driver's shouting voice or hear the crack of his heavy whip held in his warmly gloved hand.

And then, late on the afternoon of January 31, 1889, the fourth day after leaving Ontario, the driver stopped at the top of a long, steep incline to rest the sweating horses. Joel saw him point his whip toward the wide valley floor.

"Yonder's Harney Valley and Burns," he called to the weary, shivering passengers. "Won't be much longer now till we'll be there. Reckon you'll all be glad too, after bein' shook up considerable over these rough roads."

"Harney Valley!" exclaimed Joel. How often during the journey he had pictured this new land according to his father's summertime description. All the way he had thought of Father's words: "Its valley floors are covered with lush green grass that in summertime stretches upward as high as a horse's belly. Its fields lie ripe with rich grain harvests in the irrigated regions. Its nearby hills are covered with rimrock and sagebrush, and its distant mountains are covered with fine timber."

"Why, I'd forgotten that at this season of the year the valley floor would be covered by deep winter snow. Look, in places it has drifted right over the fence tops," exclaimed Joel.

"Well, shore, son," laughed the driver. "Did you expect to drive for four long days through nothin' but snow and then wind up your trip by plungin' down hill into a warm green valley?

"Harney Valley's a wonderful place, shore an' certain. But it isn't quite able yet to turn the seasons out of the natural order of things. So when it's winter up on this here hill, it's winter down there in the valley too."

"Of course it w-would be," stammered Joel. He felt his ears burn with embarrassment at his stupid remark. "I was just—well, I was just thinking about my father's description of this country. I've been thinking about it so hard ever since I left England that somehow I just expected to open my eyes and see it all there before me according to Father's description."

"Don't feel bad 'cause I laughed, son," added the kindly stage driver. "It won't be many months until you'll see it just that-a-way too. And what's more, you'll see wild game by the thousands: deer an' antelope herds, ducks, geese, quail. Oh, it's a settler's paradise for certain. You can't go wrong by comin' to Harney Valley to live."

Joel drew a long breath and rested his tired body against the hard wooden back of the seat. Steadily he gazed across the waiting miles to the small settlement of Burns. He saw that the setting sun glinted redly upon tiny, distant windowpanes, and, in spite of his former eagerness to arrive, he felt his heart sink as low as did the sun over the rounded western hills.

Suddenly Joel felt himself touched by a strange sadness that he could not shake off. He felt himself to be an object hung in empty space, having neither a beginning nor an end. He felt far, far away from all that was near and dear and familiar.

"It's a long, long way to England and to Mother and John," he thought over and over again. "What if I don't like this country? What if Father isn't glad I came? How could I go back to Goonhavern when I have no money?"

Question after question buzzed through his aching head. He longed for Mother and the comforting sound of her voice at evening worship.

And then at last the driver roared "Whoa." Joel heard the heavy wheels grind to a stop. He heard the stage doors open and listened to a deep, excited voice asking, "Well, have you got a passenger for me? I'm looking for a young lad from England."

"Father!" exclaimed Joel. From his high perch he stared down into the bearded face below. "I'm up here on top. Here I am, Father."

Feeling stiff and cold and tired, Joel awkwardly clambered down. Awkwardly he reached out toward his father's enveloping embrace. But now through his veins ran a warm, singing gladness that filled him with happiness and a deep joy in his coming.

"You're here at last, my boy. You're here at last," choked Father. "It—it's *good* to see you, son. Oh, but it's good to see you."

"And it's good to be with you, Father," replied Joel confidently. He looked about him at the laughing passengers and the village lights that now seemed to glow with a cheery welcome. Last of all he looked at his father's glad smile and shining eyes.

"It's been a long, long journey from Cornwall, England, to Oregon's cattle country," he said. "But it's wonderful to be here with you in America. Thank you, Father, for bringing me to Harney Valley."

3

Hobbled Horses

I WONDER just what day Mother left New York," Joel thought anxiously. "If her ship was late, she couldn't possibly reach Huntington on time. I may have to lay over there for several days and wait for her.

"My, I'm certainly anxious to see her again. It's been nine months since I left England. But it seems more like ninety after eating my own cooking all during that time. It'll surely be mighty fine to taste Mother's good food once more. I don't see how Father's managed to get along without her all these years."

As Joel sat in the slow-moving freight wagon behind the team of heavy horses his thoughts ran busily ahead of him. Mentally he retraced his long journey, his doubts concerning his new home, and his joy upon his arrival in Harney Valley.

"Why, it's the best thing that ever happened to me," Joel said to himself. "Of course, our log cabin isn't much of a house compared with the neat little home we rented in Goonhavern. But Mother'll soon have everything as cozy as can be. And Father's promised to build another room or so for her as soon as possible.

"The best part of all, however, is the land we own. After the tiny rented space we had in our English village this big homestead seems like half a continent! Won't Mother be surprised when she learns exactly how much property and cattle we already own?

"Father bought 160 acres right along the Silvies River, just two miles from Burns. He paid only three dollars an acre, too. Already we have thirty-five head of our own cattle grazing there. The wild hay's as tall and thick as Father said it would be.

"And won't Mother be surprised when we tell her that Father's been road supervisor all summer? With our hay crops, cattle, and his extra road salary we're better off than we've ever been.

"The best part to her will be the food, I know. Now she won't have to go to the store every time she wants a bite to eat—not with beef cattle, a milch cow, and the Barred Rock laying hens Father intends to buy when she gets here.

"Oh, this is a great country, all right. It's a country where anyone who really wants to work can make something of himself. And that's exactly what I intend to do."

Joel's thoughts were so busy that the long, slow, six-day journey from Burns to Huntington seemed to pass like a pleasant dream. He liked the noonday stop, when he would drop the bits from the horses' mouths and give them grain in their nose bags and water in a bucket. He liked the crisp September mornings, and the evenings that cooled quickly in the high, desert plateau-land of eastern Oregon. He liked his solitary meal beside the campfire at night and his snug, warm bed in the big covered wagon, which looked like a small white speck in the sagebrush vastness.

"Mother can sleep in the wagon on the way back," he thought. "I'll roll up in my blankets and stretch out underneath the wagon bed. That way I'll keep the early morning dew from wetting my bedding. I can arrange our groceries so that there'll still be room enough for the feather bed I'm sure she'll bring.

"Well, it's been a good trip. And there's Huntington right ahead. Now the first thing is to find out when Mother's train is due. Then I'll see whether she's on it! I'll hurry right over to the depot."

"You say the train's already in so early in the morning?" Joel questioned anxiously a few moments later. "But—but my mother's letter said she wouldn't get here until afternoon and—well, now I'll have to wait over a whole day at least. Perhaps she won't arrive for several days."

"Oh, I can see why you're so mixed up," smiled the friendly ticket agent in the railroad depot, as he peered through the bars of the small ticket window. "I guess your mother didn't know about the change in the train schedule until too late to let you know.

"Sorry, young man, but that train came in several hours ago and, as you can see, there's no one here but those two old codgers visiting together over in the corner. And I'm safe in saying that neither one of them looks like your mother, or anybody's mother, for that matter!"

Joel had to smile at the man's hearty laugh and his gesture toward the bearded old-timers sitting near the depot's potbellied stove.

"No, they don't," he agreed. "But I wish one of them was. I'm certainly anxious to see her. It's been nine months since I left England, and right now it seems like nine years."

Joel felt that indeed he'd give a great deal to be able to see his little mother's laughing blue eyes beneath the waving hair and glimpse the cheering smile that had never failed to encourage him.

"From England, you say?" exclaimed the ticket agent. "Why, from your own accent I should have known you'd be looking for the little lady who came up to this window just after the train pulled in.

"She walked right up here and said, 'I'm a stranger, and I'm looking for my boy. He's coming for me all the way from Burns. Can you tell me, please, if a young lad's been asking for his mother?' Why, of course, that's your mother. She's a mighty nice little lady too. No wonder you're anxious to see her again."

"Oh, she's here!" gasped Joel excitedly. "But—but where is she, then?"

"Why, she went one block down the street to the rooming and boarding house there. It's clean and respectable, and I thought it'd be a good place for her to wait in case she had to stay overnight. Of course, after the change in train schedule she didn't know when you'd be likely to get here.

"It does seem mighty strange that you two reached this little stopping-off place so close together. It seems extra strange, since your mother traveled so many thousands of miles from one direction and you came by freighter from the other direction." The station agent shook his head wonderingly. "Looks as though it was just meant to be!"

"It was!" Joel called over his shoulder as he thanked the man and hurried out the door and down the dusty street to the boardinghouse.

"Trust Mother to make everything come out all right," he exclaimed joyfully. Quickly he ran up the steps and threw his arms around the little woman who rushed to meet him.

"The station agent couldn't figure out the answer!" he explained. "But I knew the secret! I knew you'd been praying, Mother."

"That's right, my boy," nodded Mother. "I was! I've always said that all the rough spots along life's road can always be smoothed out by prayer. All through the years I've asked our heavenly Father to help us. Sometimes the clouds have been so dark I wondered if the sun would ever shine through. But I've never stopped praying.

"And look! Doesn't the fact that at last we're here in this wonderful America prove that God *will* help us? Why, I didn't lose even one wink of sleep when I knew the train schedule had been changed. I just said my prayers and left everything in His care."

Joel felt that he could never ask questions fast enough nor listen carefully enough to his mother's replies. He had chafed at the necessary delay while he took Father's grocery list to the store and helped load the household provisions in the big farm wagon with the white wagon sheet stretched over the bows. Though he longed to be hearing more news from England, he again carefully checked the long list of supplies and read aloud the last few items:

> 2 five-gallon drums of Tea Garden Syrup
> 2 wooden boxes crackers—16 pounds each
> 1 sack dried beans
> Dried fruit (apricots, prunes, apples, peaches)
> Tapioca
> Sago
> 50-pound bag granulated sugar
> 1 tin of block sulphur matches
> Coil of ½-inch hemp rope

"I guess that's all, Mother," he said cheerily. "Now we're ready to start for Harney Valley. I left a quantity of wheat at John Day. It'll be ground into flour by the time we return. We'll pick it up and also get several boxes of those fine John Day apples."

"Apples!" exclaimed Mother. "How will you keep eating apples in this cold climate during the winter months? They won't be good to eat after they're frozen."

"Oh, they can't freeze," laughed Joel. "Just wait until you see our cellar at home. It's about as wide as our bedroom back in Cornwall, and it's ten feet high. Father dug down about three feet into the ground for the floor and built up three feet into the air to support the rounded dirt-covered roof, which was four feet thick.

"It has a dirt floor, with bins for potatoes built snugly against the walls and with wide shelves where we'll lay the apples one layer deep. If necessary, we can cover them with straw so they won't freeze.

"You'll find it cool enough in there in summer so that meat can be kept safe from spoilage. You'll soon discover that the neighboring ranchers have quite a system for sharing food. One man will butcher a fat heifer and give the forequarters and one hindquarter to nearby ranch friends. He'll keep one hindquarter for himself. Some families keep a hindquarter for frying and a forequarter for boiling."

"My, I should think he'd have a hard time getting rid of that much food," marveled Mother.

"A hard time!" exclaimed Joel. "Not the way those ranchers eat! You should see a regular eastern Oregon ranch breakfast. There'll be steak, fried or warmed-over potatoes, sourdough biscuits or real light bread, butter, and cooked dried fruit with scalded cream."

"Well, that sounds like a real meal," laughed Mother. "When I cook I'll add some pasties and some English currant cake, though, and some gooseberry pie in season. I expect some Cornish dishes will also taste good."

Late afternoon twilight lay across the high plateau before Joel realized that darkness was very near. Quickly he called "Whoa" to the horses as he looked into the purpling dusk.

"We'd better stop right here, Mother," he said. "I was so busy visiting with you that I almost forgot there's no real twilight in this country. It'll soon be dark.

"This seems to be as good a spot as any to make camp. I'll pull over to the side of the road and unharness and hobble the horses. It'll not take long to start a crackling fire with some of this sagebrush. Then while you fix supper I'll feed the team."

"My, you're right about the hot fire," said Mother a few minutes later as she put the iron frying pan over the glowing coals. "But you forgot to mention the peculiar fragrance of the sage. It's unlike anything I've ever——

"Oh! What's that?" she gasped. Joel saw his tiny mother's startled face and her wide-open eyes.

"Yip. Yip. Yip. Yieeeeeee. Yip. Yip. Yip. Yieeee." The plaintive wail floated across the dark lonely miles, rising higher and higher until it broke and fell in a sobbing cry.

"Joel!" cried Mother. "That—what—do you have a gun?"

"It's all right, Mother," Joel hastened to say. "I forgot to tell you about the coyotes. You'll hear them often from now on."

"Coyote?" questioned Mother. "What a nerve-shattering cry! Is it an animal like a wolf?"

"A coyote is often called a prairie wolf," explained Joel. "But since it weighs only about thirty pounds, it's much smaller than the timber wolf. You'll probably see several of them tomorrow, and you'll notice that the coyotes in this region have grayish-colored fur, sometimes tipped with black.

"I've learned that the coyote is very cunning. He's also very clever in avoiding the poisoned meat and the traps put out for him by the cattlemen and sheep-herders."

"But why would ranchers put out poisoned bait?" questioned Mother, busying herself once more with supper preparations. "Surely such a small animal couldn't do much harm. Doesn't he live mostly on rabbits or mice?"

"Yes, he does," nodded Joel, "and he also eats gophers and birds that nest on the ground. But in the winter, when this smaller game is scarce, the coyote packs kill cattle and sheep and even hunt the pronghorn antelope. They're such bold fellows they'll sneak into a rancher's poultry house and carry away some nice fat chickens or turkeys.

"You can be sure the coyote is heartily disliked by all the ranchers, even though he's afraid of man."

"Well, I'm thankful I wasn't alone out here when I first heard that eerie bark," chuckled Mother. "I'd probably have dived head first into the wagon and stayed there, shivering and shaking.

"But here! The potatoes and eggs are done to a turn. Get your plate and I'll serve you. I'm hungry too. I guess this keen air must have sharpened my appetite. It's also made me sleepy. My eyes feel so heavy that I can scarcely hold them open."

"Well, your bed's all made for you in the wagon, Mother," Joel answered between appreciative bites of the delicious-tasting hot food.

"I'll clean up these few dishes, just to show you how good a housekeeper I've become since arriving in America.

"You go on and get ready for the night, and I'll do the same in just a few minutes. I'll roll up in my bedding and sleep underneath the wagon. At daybreak I'll get up and build the campfire. We must get an early start tomorrow, for we've a long way to go, and the wagon's heavily loaded. We'll be doing well to travel twenty miles a day."

Joel was sure his tired head had only touched the ground when the first faint light in the eastern sky roused him.

"Ho-hum!" he yawned. He stretched sleepily before he sat up and rubbed his eyes. "I guess Mother's still resting, and I'll not call her until breakfast's ready. She's had a long, hard journey, and she's feeling the need of a good rest.

"First of all I'll tend to the horses. They'll probably be glad to get those hobbles off. They didn't seem to like them very——"

He paused, suddenly aware of the dawn's unusual stillness. He listened for the comforting sound of his horses' breathing and the creaking of the hobbles that fastened their feet together. But although he strained his ears for any familiar telltale noise, he heard nothing but the drowsy chirp of a prairie bird.

"The horses," he thought wildly. "They've been stolen. Oh, what'll I do without my horses to pull the wagon? What'll I do?"

He flung back the blankets and pulled on his boots. Then, putting on his coat and cap, he rolled hurriedly from underneath the wagon's protecting dryness into the dewy roadside grass.

"Here, Boy. Here, Boy," he called over and over to his favorite horse. Though his eyes frantically scanned the horizon for some sign of his vanished team, only the quiet landscape met his searching gaze.

"Joel! What is it?"

He whirled toward the wagon as he heard his mother's worried voice.

"What's happened? Are you ill?" Again he heard his mother's anxious call.

"It's the team, Mother," he replied quickly. "They've wandered a short distance away. They can't have gone far, because they're securely hobbled.

"Don't worry. I'll soon find the fat scalawags and bring them back. I'll start searching as soon as I chop some sagebrush for a fire. I'll leave you plenty of fire-wood, and you'll be cozy as can be.

"No, thanks. I won't take time to eat! I'll not be gone long, and you can have breakfast ready for me when I get back. Good-by, Mother. Don't worry. I'll be all right."

Later on Joel was to smile ruefully as he recalled his brave leave-taking. But during the long hours that followed he grew tired and hungry and thirsty as he trudged across the dusty desert in a vain search for his vanished team.

"I don't know what I'm going to do," he choked. He felt almost overcome by the blazing sun's afternoon heat and the thick dust clouds and his own anxiety.

"Here I am, miles from somewhere, and the horses are probably just as many miles from nowhere. I don't know in which direction to turn, and yet I *can't* go back to the wagon without my team.

"It may be some time before any other traveler passes this way. I can't keep Mother waiting along the road-side. She's probably worried half to death right this minute, not for herself but for me. Oh, what *can* I do?"

As Joel stared despairingly toward the rays of the slanting sun he seemed to hear his little mother's voice. "All through the years I've asked our heavenly Father to help us. Sometimes the clouds have been so dark I wondered if the sun would ever shine through. But I've never stopped praying. . . . God *will* help us if we're only faithful."

"Mother's right," Joel murmured to himself as he bent his head and asked for help in this trying hour. "I don't know how my prayer could be answered, for I'm miles from civilization, but surely the Lord can send help today just as He did in days of old."

"Halloo there, stranger," called a loud voice. Joel opened his eyes in astonishment and turned quickly at the unexpected greeting.

"Why—where—how," he stammered. "I didn't see——"

"Of course you didn't," interrupted the bearded stranger. "My name's Wright, and I live off yonder in that direction. That's where I was a-headin' when I seen some stray horses roamin' over the hills. They was wearin' hobbles too. Then I just happened to look this way and there you was, standin' still. If you'd gone a little further over that hill, I'd sure enough have missed seein' you."

"Those surely must be my lost horses," exclaimed Joel. "I've been looking for them until I'm about worn out from walking. But I'll never be able to understand how they got this far with hobbles on their feet."

"Well, son," drawled the smiling stranger, "I don't blame you for bein' real surprised when you woke up and found no team near your camp. I had to learn the hard way too. But it only took one lesson to teach me that hobbled horses get right smart, and they soon learn to run with their hobbles fastened on. So from now on I shouldn't be one mite surprised but what you'll stake the ornery critters out too. Am I right?"

"You certainly are!" exclaimed Joel. "But what worries me is how I'm going to find them. I left my mother at our wagon hours ago, but I can't go back without my team."

"Well, I'll tell you what I thought," said the kindly rancher. "You get up here behind me, and we'll ride over to my place. It ain't far away. Then I'll loan you a horse and enough rope so's you can catch each runaway and bring him back to my place. 'T won't take too long on horseback, for they can't have gone too far since I last caught sight of 'em."

As they rode along, Joel thankfully stretched his tired legs and wriggled his cramped, aching toes. He felt that he had never had a softer, more comfortable seat than the one he now occupied on the bony back of the man's jogging mare.

"Well, Mother's certainly right!" he thought over and over again. "And if anybody ever was a good Samaritan, this man is one. I can never be thankful enough for his help."

Joel found that the next few hours sped by as rapidly as the previous ones had dragged. Even so, it was midnight when he rode wearily up to the lonely campsite and looked anxiously toward the big white-topped wagon now silvered by September moonlight.

"There's the wagon all safe and sound," he thought anxiously. "But where's Mother? There's no sign of a campfire. Surely she wouldn't have wandered away looking for me!"

Joel felt his heart pound hard as he rode toward the front of the freighter and peered eagerly into its dim depths. He felt weak with relief when his loud call was answered.

"Mother, where are you?" he asked quickly.

"I'm right here, son," answered Mother's calm, quiet voice. "I figured you'd keep on going until you found those stray horses, even if it took you a couple of days. So after I ate an early supper I just undressed and got into bed. Somehow the coyotes didn't sound quite as close as they did when I was out there by the campfire."

"O Mother," stammered Joel. "I-I'm so sorry that you had such a long wait. I-it was all my fault. I should have known that those horses needed to be securely tied."

"No harm's done except that you're tired and hungry," Mother replied. "We'll get on our way again early in the morning, and this time surely nothing will go wrong. We'll reach Burns safely. Father'll be waiting to greet us and welcome me to our new home. That's going to be wonderful!

"Oh, we've much to be thankful for, Joel. God has been very good to us."

As he heard his mother's tender words Joel swallowed hard against the lump in his throat. And then, as he saw her step down from the wagon and start toward the pile of sagebrush wood he laughed joyously at her next statement.

"But right now, my boy, just as soon as you kindle a fire, I'm going to warm up some food. After all, you told me to have breakfast ready when you got back. And since almost twenty hours have gone by, I think you've waited long enough.

"Hurry and tend your team and then come back here. We'll not waste a minute. Any boy who's been chasing hobbled horses from dawn to dark deserves a fine meal.

"I hope it'll be only the first of the many good, nourishing meals I'm planning on preparing for all of you. For soon John will come here to join us. Once again our family will be together. Somehow I feel that we can look forward to many happy years in our home in Harney Valley."

"I'm sure that's true, Mother," Joel answered. And as he looked from the moon-silvered wagon across the dim, dreaming desert his heart sang with happy thoughts of the bright future that now emerged before him.

4
Pawnee Pony

DUST! Dust! And more dust!" groaned Candace. She felt her nose smart and her eyes burn as thick, choking clouds of prairie dust rose around her and hid the creaking covered wagons from view. She sneezed violently as Jones, the black-bearded rear guard, rode past them on his way to the front of the wagon train.

"I'm tired of walking almost all the way to Oregon, aren't you?" she grumbled to her younger sister, Alicia. "Day after day we've trudged along beside our wagon until I've swallowed enough dirt to—well, to plant a garden."

"Ker-choo!" She sneezed again as she swung her heavy red braids over her shoulders and settled her faded sunbonnet more firmly on her curly hair.

" 'T wouldn't be so bad if something really exciting would happen," she continued wearily. "But already we've traveled miles and miles, and nothing unusual has happened to us. We just get up at daybreak, cook break-

50

fast over the campfire, wash the dishes, and start out once more along the Oregon Trail. Then we make camp again in the evening, eat, do the chores, and fall into bed.

"On good days we travel ten or twelves miles. On bad days we travel two or three miles. I thought it would really be exciting to go so far across the United States. But till now it's been as dull as dishwater."

"Well, maybe we're lucky that it *has* been dull," Alicia replied. "I'm sure *I* wouldn't want to meet any Indians on the warpath. And I shouldn't think you'd want to, either. I expect they'd really like to take your hair for a trophy."

"Ugh!" shuddered Candace. "Don't talk like that. I can't picture my long red braids swinging from some Indian's belt."

"Just the same, such things have happened to some of the poor people crossing the plains," Alicia replied solemnly. "And I don't suppose those folks expected an Indian raid, either."

"You're right, sister," smiled Candace with her usual good humor. "I should just be thankful that Pa and Ma and all of us are together and that little Edgar's getting better every day. He certainly was sick with that fever for a while. From now on I'm going to try to stop grumbling and appreciate my blessings."

All morning the long train had wound over the bare, dusty hills of the Great Plains region. The Parsonses' wagon occupied a place toward the rear, where the dust nearly blinded these travelers. Already Candace and Alicia felt tired and dirty and travel worn, for days had gone by since their departure. Each morning and each evening they longed for a plentiful supply of water in which to bathe. And at every hour of the day they longed for fresh, cold water to drink.

But both girls well knew that every ounce of the precious liquid in the storage barrels must be used sparingly until they reached the next water hole. They knew that the needs of the tired oxen must be considered even before the needs of their human owners, for without oxen to pull their wagon they would lose all their carefully packed possessions.

The girls talked now of some of the cherished keepsakes that unfortunate travelers had abandoned along the trail.

"Don't you wish we could have brought that little rosewood rocking chair we saw last week?" Candace asked wistfully. "It looked just right for comfortable sitting by a fireplace."

"Yes, and that chest of drawers we saw yesterday would have matched it mighty well," nodded Alicia. "We could certainly use all the furniture we've seen along the way. We won't have much when we get to Oregon. All we could bring was Grandma's rocker and Ma's melodeon, and Pa says he'll have to take them out of the wagon if we ride very much of the distance."

"That's just why I'm walking. Why, I'd even—I'd carry that melodeon if I had to. What would we do without music when we get to Oregon?" cried Candace. "Pa can cut down some of those big trees we've heard about and build a cabin from them. He can make furniture, too—furniture that'll be good enough for our log house. But he certainly couldn't build a melodeon

that'd play sweet, soft music. And I just couldn't bear
the thought of not hearing any music when we get way
out there. It'd——"

Candace stopped abruptly as she turned her head
toward the rear. Her eyes widened, and her face paled
until its freckles stood out like little brown polka dots.
Quickly she grabbed Alicia's calico sleeve.

"Look!" she breathed. "D-do you see what I see?"

"What? Where?" gasped Alicia fearfully. She looked
all around her. "I don't see anything. Do you?"

"Look back of us—way back on that little knoll we
passed some time ago. Don't you see two or three small
black specks moving across the top of the hill?"

"N-no—Yes! I do. There they go. And two or three
more right behind them," Alicia cried. "O Candace,
what do you suppose they could be? There isn't another
wagon train within miles of us. I heard our captain
talking to Pa this morning, and that's what he told him.

" 'No other wagon train's within a couple of days'
journey, Parsons,' he said. 'We'll have to keep our eyes
peeled for any stray Injuns who might be in these here
parts. I reckon they could make it mighty uncomfortable
for us.' Oh, do you suppose those could be Indians?"

"I don't know," Candace said quickly. "But I'm
going to tell Pa. There's no guard back here right now,
and somebody ought to send word to the front of the
line. Pa'll tend to that after we speak to him. If those
are Indians, we'd better be ready for most anything.
No telling what they might do."

Candace tried to speak bravely. But her voice shook
as she hurriedly called to her father.

"Pa. O Pa! Look back there. Do you see those little specks? Do you think they might be Indians?" she called.

"Whoa-a-a-p! Whoa-a-ap!" Pa's deep voice rang out as he slowed the lumbering oxen to a halt and jumped over the wagon's high wheel.

"What'd you say, daughter?" he questioned. He shaded his keen eyes with his calloused hand as he squinted into the distant horizon. "Don't know's I can rightly say what those could be," he began. "I'd be more willing to trust your say-so. You always did have eyes as sharp as an eagle's.

"But if those are Pawnees we'd better keep a good lookout. I doubt whether they'd try to harm us. Pawnees don't do much killing, but they'd sure try to steal us blind if they got a chance. I'd better get word up to our captain, so we'll all be ready if any of those redskins come riding by.

"Here's Jones now," he continued. "We'll let him take our message up front. In the meantime we'll get on our way so's we can catch up with our wagon train. I've got no hankerin' to be left alone out here on the prairie!"

"What'd Pa mean about the Pawnee Indians stealing from us?" quavered wide-eyed Alicia. "I don't see how they could steal anything in broad daylight and with everyone watching them. Do you? How *could* they?"

"I—I don't exactly know," replied Candace. "I've heard Pa and some of the men talk about them, though. They said that it'd go hard with any lone traveler who met any of the young Pawnee braves out prowling around. They wouldn't kill the traveler, but they'd probably steal his horse and all of his clothes, too."

"His horse? And his *clothes?*" queried Alicia unbeliev-ingly. "Why in the world would the Indians want his clothes?"

"Pa says a young brave steals so he can give these things as gifts to the father of his bride-to-be," explained Candace. "He hasn't anything of his own to start out with, and so he tries to steal from other tribes. But if he finds a lone white man, he takes all this traveler's belongings, and feels very rich indeed.

"But I can't talk any more now," panted Candace. "I—I'm all out of breath from walking so fast to catch up with our wagon. Pa's really hurrying the oxen as much as he can."

Candace and Alicia watched anxiously as the wagons formed a wide, unbroken circle, and the tired travelers made hasty camp. They knew that word had been passed quickly from wagon to wagon and that each family was determined to be ready should hostile Indians attack them.

Candace's fingers trembled as she helped her mother prepare the simple evening meal over their glowing camp-fire. She wished with all her heart that the small black specks she had seen earlier in the day would prove to be nothing more than buffaloes grazing on the rich green grass of the Kansas plains. But she knew that they had moved far too rapidly for grazing herds.

As she waited for bread to bake in the black Dutch oven she lifted her heavy red braids, tucked them up under her faded blue sunbonnet, and pulled its strings tight under her firm chin. She had just finished tying a bow when a shout from Jones startled the entire camp.

"Halloo! Look out, everyone! Be on guard. Here come the Pawnees!"

"Y-you w-w-were just in t-time!" shivered Alicia. "It—it's a good thing you h-hid your r-red hair. Y-you don't w-want to be s-s-scalped."

Candace opened her mouth only to have the words die on her lips. For there, riding at full speed toward them, she saw a group of young Indians. She felt her scalp prickle and her backbone tingle as the leader reined his Pawnee pony toward the camp and stopped opposite the Parsonses' wagon, right in front of Candace.

She watched, spellbound, as the leader of the group began talking in sign language with Jones, the rear guard. She listened carefully as Jones translated the Indian signs for Pa and the other men, who, with their rifles in their hands, stood warily inside the wagon circle, ready for any hostile move on the part of their visitors.

"He says he's been traveling for over a moon, and met these other Indian braves only a short time ago," Jones said to his fellow emigrants. "He says he means no harm to any of us and for us not to be afraid. He and his Indian friends are on their way home. They are empty-handed after a hunting raid.

"He says they are only passing by our wagon train, and that they will soon be out of sight. It's my own guess they'll not bother us unless they see something they really want, and we don't have any——"

"Get back, Edgar. Get back!"

Candace and Alicia jumped and turned startled eyes toward the rear of their wagon as Pa's sharp tones rang out.

"O Edgar! Get back inside," cried Candace. She shivered with fear as she saw the Pawnee brave's quick admiring gaze at her little brother's laughing face and his flaming red curls.

"Get in the wagon with your ma," commanded Pa, striding toward his small son. "And stay there!" he added sternly. Candace saw his lips tighten in a straight, firm line and knew that he too was worried.

"Well, there they go!" exclaimed Jones. They watched as the Indians wheeled their horses and dashed away across the rolling Kansas swells.

"And we're all right!" cried Candace. "They didn't harm any of us after all. We're safe. Oh, we're all safe."

"We're safe enough right now," soberly added Pa. "But I wouldn't say as to what might happen later on. I didn't know much of their lingo as they talked. But I'm a pretty good judge of a man's face, and I didn't like the shifty look in that redskin's eyes.

"Mark my words. He's up to some sort of trickery. We'll have to be on our guard every minute of the day and night or he'll try and slip something over on us."

"You're right, Parsons," nodded Jones. "We'll have to double our guard duty tonight, especially with the cattle and horses. Those Pawnees are clever enough to steal a horse right out from under your very legs and leave you wondering how they did it!

"Come on, men. Let's post guards right now. No telling what'll happen!"

"Oh, do you think they'll come back?" Candace heard Alicia's frightened murmur. "Wh-what'll we do, Candy? What'll we do?"

"Now, now," soothed Candace. "Don't you worry. Pa'll see that our wagon's taken care of, and the other men'll look to their own wagons. You heard what Mr. Jones said about those Indians. They aren't on the war-path at all. They're just looking around for something easy to steal. But they didn't find anything here, so they went peaceably away.

"Now do quit worrying about it and get into the wagon. You know you promised you'd tell Edgar a story if he was a good boy today.

"You'd better hurry so we can all get to sleep. Ma needs her rest, especially since she was up so many nights with Edgar when he was sick. And tomorrow we'll get an early start, Pa said. He wants to put as many miles as he can between us and those Pawnee Indians."

Candace was sure she couldn't get to sleep, although she was so tired that she could scarcely wait to take off her dress and shoes, say her prayers, and slip into bed. Almost instantly she closed her eyes and drifted into deep slumber. She roused only once when little Edgar stirred uneasily and rolled in his warm blankets toward the wagon's endgate.

"Come! Come back, Edgar," she tried to command, only half opening her heavy eyelids. But at once she again fell into a deep sleep, from which she did not awaken until early morning. Even the wild commotion caused by a midnight Indian alarm seemed only a troubled dream to the trail-weary girl.

The east was faintly pink when Candace opened her eyes, yawned, and then sat up quickly. She shivered in the chill of the early morning air.

"Br-r-r!" she whispered as she poked snoring Alicia with her forefinger. "Wake up. Ma and Edgar are still asleep, but Pa's got the campfire going. We'd better get dressed and start breakfast. We'll let the folks rest until we're ready to eat. Then we'll call them."

"Oooh," moaned Alicia. "I'm so tired I could lie in bed for a week. But I'll get up so we can hurry and move on. Wasn't that noise awful last night? I was so frightened, I——"

"Noise? What noise?" questioned Candace sharply. "I dreamed I heard the Indians and Pa and all the men yelling back and forth at each other. But when I raised up, everything was quiet, and Edgar was rolled up in his blankets just like he is now.

"Sh! Don't wake him. He'll get up as soon as he smells breakfast cooking. Trust him to know when it's time to eat!"

"All right, I'm dressed," murmured Alicia. "Let's hurry. But you weren't dreaming. Those Indians *did* come back last night. They tried to steal some of our horses and cattle. They didn't stop near us, but I heard Pa start out with his gun, and it was quite a little while before he came back. I thought I heard him near our wagon, but by that time I was so scared I just put my head under the covers and my hands over my ears. And then I guess I went back to sleep, because all at once it was morning."

"And to think I was such a sleepyhead I missed all the excitement," mourned Candace. "Here I've been wishing something different would happen, and when it does I'm sound asleep."

"Breakfast!" she called a few minutes later.

"Coming!" answered Ma. "I'll be there just as soon as I wake Edgar. Poor baby. He's tired out but——

"Help! Help! Pa! Get help!"

Candace dropped the iron spider and began running toward the wagon the instant she heard her mother's frantic scream.

"What is it, Ma?" she called over and over. "What's happened? Are you sick?"

"No, no. It's Edgar. It's our baby," moaned Mother.

"Edgar?" Candace heard Pa's deep voice over her shoulder. "Is he worse?"

"He's not sick," cried Ma. "He—he's gone." She leaned against Pa's broad chest and burst into frightened tears.

"Gone!" Pa exclaimed. "Why, how could he get away? He must be here near the wagon."

"No. No, he isn't," wailed Ma. "Look how cleverly his blankets were rolled up to look just as though he were sleeping in them. But they're cold. He hasn't been in them for hours. Those thieving Indians have stolen him. I know they have! Oh, my baby. My baby. I'll never see him again!"

Candace felt her heart plunge sickeningly downward. Again she recalled the vivid dream of the past night. Again she heard the stealthy approach of the Indians, the whispered command, and Edgar's quickly stifled cry. She swallowed hard and winked back the tears as she despairingly realized that Alicia had been right and that the kidnaping had been no dream. All this had really happened. Little Edgar was a prisoner of the Indians.

"O Pa—wh-what'll they do with Edgar?" she cried. "Will they—will they kill him?"

"I don't know, child. I don't know!" groaned Pa. "We can only hope and pray as we get our horses and start after them."

"Let me go too, Pa. Please let me go," Candace begged. "I can ride as good as any of the men. You know I can, Pa. And maybe I can help find Edgar. Why, you've always called me Sharp-Eyes. Maybe I'll see something no one else would notice."

"No, child, no," replied Pa. "I couldn't let you start out on such a chase. Why, no telling where we'll go or what'll happen before we get back. There might be shooting. I'd never forgive myself if anything happened to you too.

"Here's Jones now. All ready? We won't need that extra horse, Jones. Ned's already saddled up his roan. Just tie the reins here to our wagon and let's be off. We can't waste another minute. Right now time's more precious than gold.

"Take good care of Ma and Alicia," Pa shouted back to Candace. "And keep on praying that we'll find our boy."

"I can't—I won't stay here," gasped Candace. She whirled toward the saddled and bridled bay mare. "I can ride as fast as any of the men. And I just know I can find Edgar, too. You look out for Ma, Alicia. Make her lie down and rest as much as she can.

"I've never disobeyed Pa before, but I've just got to now. Somehow I've got a feeling I can find Edgar when no one else can."

Without the loss of another second, Candace jumped into the saddle, slapped the reins across the mare's neck, and galloped after Pa and the men from the wagon train. She set her teeth tightly against the horse's jolting motion and clung grimly to the saddle horn as the mare stumbled and regained her footing.

She braced herself for Pa's anger when she overtook the riders. But she knew that Pa would never dare to send her back to the wagon train alone. She knew, too, that none of the riders could turn back now when little Edgar's life hung in the balance.

On and on. Ker-lip! Ker-lip! Ker-lip! sounded the horses' hoofs. On and on. Candace's heavy braids bounced up and down, up and down. On and on the pursuers rode. And then, as they slowed their horses for a brief rest, her sharp eyes caught a movement just to their right. Intently she stared, shading her eyes against the brightness of the rising sun.

"Look, Pa!" she cried. "There. To your right. Aren't those the Indians we're looking for?"

"Sure enough," exclaimed Pa. "You're right, daughter. And it looks like they'd had some kind of trouble with a couple of their horses. Looks as though they're lame or plumb winded, I don't know which. But before we ride up to them we'll put our guns in a position easy for these Pawnees to see.

"Get ready for a powwow, Jones. You're the only one here who understands them right well."

It seemed to Candace that hours crawled by as Jones approached the wary, waiting braves, signaled peaceably to them, and began to talk in the sign language.

"No," said Jones. "They say they've seen nothing of a small boy. Nor did they run off any of our horses during the night. They say we can see for ourselves that they have only their own horses, and nothing else, with them."

"Ask them what they did with our livestock, then," thundered Pa. "And, most important of all, ask what they did with my boy. Make them tell us the truth or I'll——"

"Easy now, Parsons," cautioned Jones. "It won't do no good to get 'em all riled up. We'll probably find our horses running loose somewhere between here and camp. But where we'll find the missing boy, I don't know. It looks suspicious, but you can see for yourself he isn't in sight.

"I'll have another try, though, for we've got to do something mighty fast. Some of us can stay behind and keep on searching, but you know as well as I do that the wagon train has got to keep moving right along. If we get behind schedule, we'll all get caught in the high mountains in wintertime, and we can't risk that.

"I'll try again to get the truth out of 'em. But stand back and be as quiet as you can while we talk."

Breathlessly Candace watched as Jones and the Pawnee brave spoke in the Indian sign language. Breathlessly she watched as the Indian shook his head and signaled his men that it was time to ride on over the distant horizon. She stared hard at the Indian's pony as he half turned to depart. And then she screamed.

"Look! O Pa! Look at that blanket roll on the back of that Pawnee pony. It—it moved. I saw it move."

"S-sh, girl," cautioned Jones. "You'll get 'em all riled up. Then we'll have trouble, sure as shootin'. Better let me handle this. There may be dozens of Pawnees a-settin' on their horses just over the brow of that hill, all ready and waitin' to ride down here and scalp us."

"I don't care," cried Candace. "I saw that blanket move! And I just know my little brother's hidden in it. I may not know your sign language, but I've got one of my own. And I'm going to use it too."

And before any of the horrified men could stop her, Candace urged her horse toward the astounded Pawnee brave. She reined to a stop by his side. White men and Indians watched wonderingly as she pointed from her long red braids to the bundle on the back of the tall Indian's pony.

"I have red hair—my little brother has red hair too. You give me back the little red-haired brother who looks like me," she said slowly and clearly.

For a long moment Candace and the Pawnee stared unflinchingly at each other. Then, to the unbelieving wonder of the emigrants, the Pawnee brave smiled. With a swift gesture he reached for the heavy blanket and lifted it in front of him. With a swifter gesture he unrolled it and brought to view a very much rumpled and frightened little redheaded boy who took one look at Candace and burst into tears of joy.

"I knew you were there," she said over and over, as she reached for him and held him close to her. "Don't cry. Sister knew she'd find you. You're all right now. Sh! Don't cry, honey."

The Indians galloped away in a cloud of dust.

"Well——" gasped Jones, as they rode triumphantly toward the waiting wagon train.

"I'd never believed it in a thousand years if I hadn't seen it with my own eyes. To think that a girl rode right up to a Pawnee brave, looked him in the eye, and got her little brother back——well!"

"It was nothing short of a miracle," Pa said solemnly. "He'd never have given up the boy to anyone but Candace. He said so in that heathenish sign talk he made with you, didn't he?

"Said he'd liked the color of our boy's hair and decided he'd steal him and adopt him into the Pawnee tribe. There he'd grow up to be a red-headed Indian chief. Guess he'd have traded his Pawnee pony for Candace, too, if we'd been willing to make a bargain with him. Said she was a brave white squaw."

"Well, his scheme would've worked too if it hadn't been for Candace. I reckon it was a mighty good thing you came along, after all, even if your Pa didn't want you to," concluded Jones.

"I didn't intend to disobey Pa," said Candace soberly. "But I just knew those Indians had Edgar. And I knew I could get him back if anyone could.

"I thought we'd be safe enough. After all, I just figured that two redheads would be too much for even a Pawnee. And I was right!"

5

The Strength of an Ox

THE COLD wind slashed across Jed's face as he hastily climbed into the borrowed cart out in front of the old log cabin. Pulling the bearskin robe up to his chin, he watched his father carry in the last armload of wood, latch the door, and hurry across the frozen ground toward him.

"Br-r-r! I'm cold," Jed said through chattering teeth. Already his nose was reddened by the frosty autumn air.

"I know you are, son," said his father. "It's a bitter day for certain, but I couldn't go without replacing the same amount of firewood as we'd used. That's the unwritten law of the trail, you know. Some poor fellow in need of warmth might come stumbling along to this same deserted cabin. Perhaps he'd be so cold that he couldn't cut wood. That very thing happened to a mail carrier near my boyhood home."

Jethro Wheeler sprang into the cart, picked up the reins, and called, "Let's go, Buck," and the old ox moved slowly but steadily forward, head down against the rising wind.

"What happened then, Father?" questioned Jed in a small voice. He waited, and after a few minutes again asked, "But what happened to the mail carrier? Couldn't he find the cabin?"

"Eh?" asked Mr. Wheeler. He turned his startled gaze upon his young son. "Oh, I'm sorry. I was watching old Buck—I don't like the way he's breathing—and I forgot all about my story.

"Well, this mail carrier had crossed the mountains many times, traveling on snowshoes. He had always made the long trip in safety, for he stopped overnight at a certain cabin shelter that he kept supplied with kindling and wood. But on this particular trip he was caught in a severe, unexpected blizzard. Hours behind schedule, he managed to stumble through the unlatched cabin door, and fell half-frozen upon the dirt floor. It was all he could do to drag himself to his knees and crawl to the fireplace where he kept the moss and kindling in readiness. But when he got there——"

"O Father," broke in Jed, "could he light the fire? Or——"

"No, son, he couldn't," Mr. Wheeler soberly replied. "For some unknown traveler had stayed overnight in the shelter, used up the wood and kindling, and left without bringing in a fresh supply. No, the poor man could have lighted a fire, but he wasn't able to go out and cut wood. It was a week before a rescue party broke trail and found him, and long before that he had frozen to death.

"But here! All this happened many years ago. I think

that we've had enough talk about freezing; we'll have ourselves chilled to the bone if we aren't careful. Pull your ear flaps down and be sure to keep your red wool muffler up around your throat. Mother will be heart-sick if you become ill again."

Jethro Wheeler glanced worriedly down at the small, huddled figure leaning against him. It had been a long, hard trip out to the nearest settlement, with the two slow oxen pulling the heavy wagon. Not even the necessity of getting much-needed supplies would have forced him to undertake the journey at this time of year, with its threat of sudden blizzards. He had made one trip early in the fall, and they could have managed until spring if necessary, although they might have had short rations before the arrival of good weather. However, little Jed, their only child, had not been well for some time. Frequently he lay in his rude bunk for days at a time, his face burning with fever, his choked voice calling for a cool drink. At last his mother, frantic with worry, had insisted that the child be taken to the nearest doctor, five days' journey by ox team.

"Well," thought Jethro grimly, "I took the boy to the doctor all right, and he gave us some medicine and some good advice that's not going to be of much help unless we soon reach shelter." His sober gaze stared straight ahead, over the broad, slowly moving back of old Buck, and he frowned worriedly as he recalled the physician's final warning before they left Little Rock settlement.

"I'm sure that the boy will be all right if you follow the treatment outlined and give him the medicine twice a day. But don't let him get chilled, whatever you do. In his weakened condition it might prove fatal. He's not strong enough to stand real blizzard weather, so be sure to keep him in where it's warm."

"Keep him in where it's warm!" Mr. Wheeler thought grimly. Already the wind had sharpened. It moaned a wild, weird song as it blew across the frozen land. A fierce gust caught Buck full face, and the tired, patient creature wavered and turned toward the left.

"Back Gee, Buck. Back Gee [come to the right], I say," he called, and sat tensely until the plodding animal again struggled forward straight into the face of the rising gale.

"Poor Buck. He misses Charley. I'm sure he does," said Jed through chattering teeth.

"Yes, son, I'm sure he does," his father nodded. "It's natural that he would. I've had them both from the time they were little calves, long before you were born." He glanced down at the child and then continued talking, more for the purpose of keeping Jed awake than anything else, for the slashing wind made talking difficult. Every sentence made him sharply draw his breath.

"Yes, I began yoking them together. Then, when they were yearlings, I branded them with our own Lazy C mark. After that I had them drag logs around the field for practice in pulling. I didn't use any harness—just a yoke and bow around the neck, and the yoke fastened to the wagon tongue by log chains. They were so well trained that they'd work together or each would work singly when fastened to a small plow. It's a good thing for us that Buck was taught to work alone. Otherwise he wouldn't pull this cart."

"And you even trained Buck and Charley so that you could ride them!" Jed added, with a small boy's admiration for his father.

"That's right. I did. They've been a mighty fine pair of oxen. They've always been so gentle that I've never had to cut off their horns. I've always given them good care and fed them well on hay, corn shucks, and ear corn.

"But now they're really too old to work. I wouldn't have driven them on this trip if I'd had time to go over to Mr. Long's and pay him the $75 he's asking for his yoke of steers. But as soon as we get home I'll not work Buck any more."

"Oh, how I wish we had our big wagon with Buck and Charley pulling it together," Jed burst forth. "Why did Charley have to hurt his leg? If he hadn't stepped in that gopher hole we'd have had all our provisions with us. We could have stayed at that old cabin and waited for the storm to blow over, for we'd have plenty of food. Now you'll have to go all the way back to Halfway House to get him and our wagon load of winter supplies!"

Round and round creaked the rickety wheels. On and on plodded the weary ox. Lower and lower sank Jethro Wheeler's heart as he bent his snow-whitened head to look at his child.

"We must go forward. We *must!* If we don't reach home tonight, it will be too late. It's getting colder and colder every minute."

Just then Buck plunged to one side and started to back track on the trail.

"Whoa come, Buck. Whoa come [come to the left]," he shouted. For once the ox did not respond to his master's voice, but stood still, head hanging low and tail turned toward the tempest.

"Let's go. Come on, Buck. Let's go [get up]," Jethro Wheeler called out. "Come on, Buck. Only a few more miles, and we'll be home. Try once more." He sprang from the cart and hurried to the side of the ox.

"What's wrong, old fellow?" he called. "I've been worried about you. What's wrong?" But even as he put his mittened hand upon the neck of the faithful beast he started back in dismay. For at that very instant Buck, worn out by his fierce exertion, dropped heavily to the snowy ground and lay there, lifeless.

"Dead. Buck's dead," Jethro Wheeler thought frantically. "What shall I do? What *can* I do!"

To attempt to carry the boy the remaining distance would be fatal, both for himself and for his child. He knew that he had not sufficient strength to carry even the lightest burden in the face of the howling gale. And it was unthinkable to expose Jed any further to the biting zero weather. Unless he could be kept warm until rescued he would surely die.

Jed's father beat his hands together as he walked around and around the sled. A dozen wild schemes flashed through his mind, only to be rejected as impractical.

"But what shall I do to save my boy? I *must* save my son."

Half-blinded by the snow and sleet, he stumbled across the still body of old Buck. And at that instant he had his answer. But could he do this thing? Would this last desperate effort save the life of his child?

For a moment he stood still, dreading the decision. Then, grim-faced, he reached into the cart, pulled out his sharp hunting knife, and set to work to open the body of the lifeless ox.

"What—what is it, Father?" whispered Jed, as he half roused to feel himself being lifted from the seat. But almost instantly his eyelids fluttered shut, and he resumed his heavy breathing.

"Listen, Jed. Listen to me," his father called desperately, shaking Jed awake. "Jed, listen to me."

"Y-es, Father? What-what is it? I'm—so sleepy. Are we home? Wh-where's mother?"

"Son, I'm going home—now—to mother. I'll come back as soon as I can get help. I can't carry you in this storm. Are you listening? Listen carefully, Jed. I'm leaving you here. Do you understand? You're to stay here!"

Now the heavy eyelids flew wide open as Jed roused and gasped, "Here? In the cold? Why, I—I'll freeze. Take me with you, Father. I'll walk. I'm sure I can walk. Only don't leave me. Please don't leave me, Father."

Never again in Jed's lifetime was he so frightened as he was at that moment, when he realized what his father had just told him. What could his father mean. He stared wildly at him.

"Listen carefully, Jed," his father repeated. "I'm going to roll you up in this robe—just like this. There. Now I'm going to leave you while I go for help, but you're not going to be cold. You're going to be in a safe, warm place. You must stay there until I return. Don't try to move. Remember, you must stay there until I come back for you. If you do as I say, you will be quite safe."

Without trusting himself to say another word he swiftly lifted Jed and carried him over to the spot where the body of old Buck lay, lifeless but warm. And then Jed understood. His father stooped and carefully placed his son inside the opened body of the ox, turning him so that he could breathe fresh air and yet covering him so that he was protected from the storm.

The old settlers still tell of that terrible early blizzard and of the almost superhuman struggle of Jethro Wheeler to reach his home. And it was the talk of the entire countryside after the rescue party retraced his steps over the weary miles to the place where he had been forced to leave his son. For there, inside the snow-covered animal, exactly as he had left him long hours before, lay Jed, safe and warm. There he lay, opening his eyes to look up into his father's eager face—saved by the strength of an ox.

6
Swift Waters

GINGER ROLLED over and opened one sleepy eye as she reached out and turned off the alarm. She had just pulled the covers up over her head when her mother spoke.

"None of that, young lady. It's time to get up! Don't you remember that today we decided to set the alarm a half hour earlier than usual so we wouldn't be late? We must be ready in plenty of time, for we may have to wait for a bus."

Virginia (Ginger) and her mother, Mrs. Leach, were spending the summer in Eugene, Oregon, where they were living in a one-room apartment in a large former fraternity home that, because of the housing shortage, had been converted into small apartments. Although it was Saturday and the large building was filled with the familiar bustle of week-day activities and the sound of children's merry voices, Ginger and her mother were not taking part in the usual tasks. For this day was the

Sabbath, and they were planning to attend church services in the large downtown Seventh-day Adventist
church.

"I'll get up right now!" cheerily answered the sixteen-
year-old girl, as she threw back the bed covers and
jumped hastily out on the rug. "I was so sleepy that at
first I thought it was time to go to work at the cleaners.
I was trying to catch a few extra winks, just as I always
did down at Lodi Academy when the rising bell sounded.
Then I realized it was Sabbath."

"Well, hurry, dear. I've laid out the clothes that you
decided to wear, and although it's August, I don't believe
that you'll be too warm if you wear your new gray coat.
Or perhaps you'd prefer to carry it over your arm. You'll
look very sweet in your new white blouse and gray skirt.
I thought you'd want your lace-trimmed slip also, so I
put it with your clothing."

She smiled proudly at her pretty daughter as they
closed their door and started down the hall. She thought
how much she and Virginia were enjoying the summer
months spent in the old, vine-covered home right on the
green banks of the tree-lined millrace—the small, swift
stream whose deep channel cut across the University of
Oregon district and on through part of the city. Many
happy evenings had been spent in fireplace "sings" with
the five or six congenial families who also lived under the
big red roof. Ginger had proved to be especially popular
with the many small children, who liked to watch her
splash and play in the cold stream, which was too deep
and too swift for them to enter.

One of the younger girls heard their footsteps and

ran to meet them. It was four-year-old Judy Luck, who loved Ginger dearly. As the older girl bent to kiss the rosy cheek, Judy exclaimed, "Oh, Gingie, you look so pretty with your new black shoes and new hat. I wish I could go with you. Could I, Gingie?"

"Not now, honey," laughed Virginia. "We thought we got up quite early, but somehow we must have slowed down, for we've just barely time to have breakfast and get to church. I don't like to be late, and today a visiting minister is speaking, so I want to be sure and hear his sermon. Some other time we'll take you and Dianne to the Sabbath school kindergarten, for they have many interesting stories and songs for little boys and girls."

"Judy, where are you?" a voice called, as Mrs. Luck came up the stairway, hairbrush in hand. "Don't look so worried, Virginia. I'm not going to spank Judy; I'm just going to brush her hair. Blonde hair seems to tangle so quickly. I had to run down to the back porch to see where Dianne was playing. She's the most fearless six-year-old I ever saw. Every day I must remind her to stay away from the water's edge. It's swift even for a good swimmer like you. It makes me shudder to think what would happen if a child fell in."

Virginia waved good-by to Judy as she and her mother hurried downstairs to the big community kitchen where each family prepared meals. Four women were already there, and for a few minutes everyone visited in the cheerful breakfast room. Then one of the women stepped out onto the porch for a minute but returned almost instantly. "Quick—quick. Help her! She's out there——" she gasped, almost too frightened to speak.

"Why, what's happened!" exclaimed Virginia, as she ran to the woman's side. "Who is out there? You are as white as a sheet! Here, sit down in this chair. I'll get you a glass of water."

"No—no," the frightened woman gasped as she pushed Virginia away. "You don't understand. Don't stop. It—it's Dianne. One of the little boys in the yard called to me. He—he said that Dianne had fallen in the millrace. Hurry!"

Quickly Virginia and her mother ran outside, with all the others following. Virginia knew that she was the only one present who could swim, and without stopping to realize her own possible danger she ran swiftly to the millrace bank.

"Wait, Ginger," her mother called. "Take off your skirt. It'll hold you back. Take it off."

Virginia paused only long enough to unfasten her waistband and step out of her gray suit skirt. Then, catching a glimpse of the drowning child, with a quick, clean-cut dive she flashed into the swift water. But just at that moment the little figure sank out of sight. The frightened onlookers wondered frantically where little Dianne could be, when all at once Mrs. Leach cried out, "Look! There she is—over by the other bank. Oh! but she is drifting away so fast that Gingie will miss her! It's too late. Too late!"

Through tear-filled eyes they stared at the small, blue-clad-figure, now drifting motionlessly away, feet first and arms outspread. They watched in frozen horror as Virginia reached the opposite bank only long enough to catch her breath. Then, as she once again caught sight of Dianne, she gave a little spring that sent her flying into the water—and momentarily she disappeared.

Mrs. Leach wondered desperately whether the mill-race would claim two victims that August day. She felt so weak and helpless that she almost fainted from terror and despair.

"If only I could do something," she thought wildly. "If only I could help my precious girl and that little child!" And then her answer came as clearly as though a voice had spoken in her ear.

"Pray!"

Pray? Why, of course. The words rang in her ears: "When thou passest through the waters, I will be with thee. . . . Fear not: for I am with thee."

Eyes fixed on the unbroken water, she prayed as she had never prayed before in her life. She knew that Gingie, somewhere in that deep channel, was even then praying to the One who had said, "If thou canst believe, all things are possible to him that believeth."

And then, four feet beyond the now barely visible Dianne, Virginia's head broke the surface of the waves.

But even then, because of the motion of the water, she did not see the little child. Mrs. Leach's lips moved silently as she stared unwinkingly toward Virginia; her fingernails pressed deep into her palms.

"There, Gingie," she kept repeating within herself. "Dianne's right there. She's near you. Oh! can't you see her—just below the surface. Look, my child. Look!"

At that very instant Dianne's little face and hands came to the surface for only a second, but that was sufficient time for Virginia to reach out in a mad lunge and grasp a handful of long blonde hair.

Next came the struggle to reach shore and the outstretched hands of the two little boys who were the only ones on that side of the stream. Dianne's little playmates dragged her up on the bank, where she lay, still and cold. The almost exhausted rescuer pulled herself up on the edge of the stream and then hurried to the three little figures dreading lest she had reached the tiny girl too late.

She ran to Dianne and turned her over on her stomach in order to give artificial respiration. But before that could be started, Dianne gasped for air, opened her eyes, and started crying. Oh, what pitiful crying! But how glad Virginia was to hear the sound. She gathered the little drenched, frightened child up in her arms and held her tight, murmuring soothing words until the women had time to run around by way of the bridge and reach them.

One of the women carried Dianne into the house, where many willing hands cared for her and for her frightened mother, who had known nothing about the near tragedy until her half-drowned child was brought into the house.

"Are you all right, dear?" Mrs. Leach asked Virginia as they sat on the bank, resting for a few moments.

"Yes, Mother, I'm all right," Virginia replied quietly. Everything seemed very peaceful and calm after the few moments of violent stress. Then the girl spoke again as she stared into the silently moving waters, and watched the little black hat with the now-wilted veil become a speck far down the stream.

"Mother, I could never have done it alone!"

Mrs. Leach nodded. She knew well what her daughter meant. Many times she had seen her play in the mill-race, but never before had she been able to go so nearly straight across that swift current. Yet with His help she had just done that very thing!

When they were once again in their room, Virginia said, "Mother, please don't tell anyone about this, will you? After all, it was no more than anyone else would have done. And I don't want people making a fuss over me!"

But in this respect her wish was not to be granted. Her picture and the story of the daring rescue appeared not only in the local paper, which carried a front-page feature story, with the statement that she was being recommended for the Carnegie Medal, but also in newspapers throughout the United States from the San Francisco *Examiner* to the New York *Times*. Several news commentators mentioned the rescue on their radio programs, and Virginia received many letters of commendation.

However, the unsought recognition which she prized the most came on Tuesday evening, August 14. Just three days after the accident, as she and her mother sat in the Eugene Hotel dining room with the Luck family, Mr. and Mrs. Luck presented her with a beautiful little rose gold wrist watch. The dinner was delicious, and everyone had a wonderful time. But best of all were the words of little Dianne and Judy, who looked at her with love and devotion shining in their eyes as they said, "We'll always love you, Ginger."

Oh, how thankful Virginia was, as she looked at little Dianne, for God's help and sustaining power.

"Yes," she thought, "it's a wonderful feeling—that of having served others. But it is even more wonderful to feel God's helping hand and to know that your prayers are being answered."

7

Wonderful George

I DON'T SEE why anyone wants to live in such a dull little town, anyway," grumbled Harold. The corners of his mouth drooped, and his sullen face was turned away from his Cousin John.

"Why, I think this is a mighty nice place," John replied. "We'll have a lot of fun. You just wait and see if we don't."

"Well, if I'd known what it would be like over here I'd never have come. But mother and dad told me it would be 'just wonderful to spend the summer at Uncle Robert and Aunt Jessie's.' It would be so much better than traveling east with them." In an ugly voice he mimicked his father.

"Pooh! I've been here over a week and we haven't done one single interesting thing." He scowled and then kicked angrily at a clod until it splattered against a pink rosebush. "In fact, we haven't done anything, except go for a few rides. I'd just about as soon be dead as have nothing to do."

Suddenly the little boys jumped and whirled about as Aunt Jessie's voice sounded gaily behind them. She had very quietly walked up while they were talking, and she had overheard Harold's complaint.

"Run in quickly, wash your hands, and comb your hair," she urged. "We're going to pay a visit to a dear friend who has just returned home from a distant city. Oh, yes. And you boys may get some library books there if you wish."

"Library books!" exclaimed Harold, who greatly liked to read. "Why, I didn't know that the city library was open. John said that we couldn't get any books for a long time—maybe all summer. He said the fire had ruined the inside of the library building and part of the books. So I——"

"Never mind," laughed cheerful Aunt Jessie. "Do as I tell you, and I will introduce you to the most interesting librarian in the country. You will always remember him after your first visit."

A few moments later the three callers walked across a smooth green lawn bordered by tall hollyhocks. They crossed a wide porch and entered the open door.

Harold's eyes darted about the huge room, with its bright sailboat wallpaper, huge stone fireplace, and white-curtained windows stretching across one entire wall. They rested upon the shelves and shelves of books —large books and small books, fat books and thin books —that were stacked on shelves from ceiling to floor. Then they stared at the brown-faced young man on the high, single bed in front of the many windows overlooking Harney Valley.

"Why, how do you do, Mrs. Moore. I'm so glad to see you once again. How are you, John? Enjoying your vacation from school? And this must be your cousin. My sister wrote that you were expecting him." The man's deep voice was pleasant, and his smile showed flashing white teeth.

Harold gazed wordlessly and made no move.

"Come on over," whispered John, pulling at his sleeve and stepping forward. "Come on!" Then he said, "Harold, this is George Hibbard."

Harold walked to the side of the bed and put out his hand. He stammered a polite "How do you do, sir."

"I'm very well, thank you, Harold, but I can't shake hands. You see, I am paralyzed from the neck down. I can move my head from one side to the other, but that is all."

"You can't even move?" Harold burst forth. "Oh, how awful! I—I'm so sorry. I didn't know——"

"That's all right, sonny. I've been explaining to strangers for so many years that now it seems quite a natural thing to do."

"For years?" echoed the newcomer, to whom one week had seemed forever and ever. "You mean that you've been in bed for years?"

"That's right. Shall I tell you what caused my accident? Perhaps it will help you to be a more careful boy. Your aunt and your Cousin John know all about this, so I am sure that they would enjoy looking at some of the new books and magazines that came in on the mail stage yesterday."

Mrs. Moore and John moved eagerly to the table

overflowing with good reading material, and Harold pulled up a chair beside Mr. Hibbard's bed and listened, wide-eyed, to the story that he told.

"One hot summer day in August, 1932, several boys and I were swimming in a deep gravel pit near town. I especially enjoyed swimming, for dad had early taught each of us eight children to love the water.

"We had decided to get out and come home, but just then one of the boys wanted to take one more plunge. I, too, thought that I would take my last dive. I climbed to a height of about twelve feet, ran and jumped, and came straight down into a hidden gravel bank under the water's edge, striking the rocks. I felt no pain, but I could not move. I floated to the surface, and when my friends saw me, face down in the water, they hurried to pull me out." He paused for a moment.

"What happened then, Mr. Hibbard?" Harold breathlessly inquired.

"Well, I was rushed to the hospital, where the doctor told my parents that I would live only a few hours. He sent for a famous specialist, who flew in a private airplane to try to save my life, for everyone thought that I would die. My life was spared, but since that time I have not been able to move my body. So you see that was in truth my last dive."

Harold swallowed, trying to speak. "But what can you do——" he began, when a telephone bell rang in the square black box fastened to the top of the bed.

"Just a moment, please, while I answer this call. I always answer all the telephone calls, and that saves my sister, Eugenia, many steps and many minutes each day.

Watch how I turn my head and press against this long lever that comes down by the pillow."

George pushed slightly against the lever, and at once the iron piece holding the receiver began to come down, ever so gently, from the head of the bed. Within a few seconds there was a sharp click and the receiver lay on the pillow, right beside the young man's ear. Harold heard a faraway voice say, "Hello," and then George answered.

When he had finished talking, his head again pushed against the lever. There was a whirring sound, and the receiver was pulled back up to the black box.

"Why, that's really wonderful!" the little boy exclaimed. "I never saw any telephone like that before."

"No, and I don't imagine that you will, for a friend of mine who is an excellent mechanic made it especially for me. As far as I know, it is the only one of its kind in all the world. You can see that I am indeed well blessed with good friends."

He smiled at Harold, who had not moved in his chair since George began talking.

"And now perhaps you would like to see some of my albums. I am very proud of them, for they contain pictures of, and letters from, several former Presidents, kings, queens, governors, famous musicians, and radio stars, and leading authors and composers. Many of the people who have written to me have stopped to see me as they traveled through Burns, and a number of them have driven many miles out of their way just to come to my home. It makes me happy to know that there are so many kind and good people in the world."

Just then Mrs. Moore and John came over to the bedside. Each carried several books.

"We have signed the library cards for these and put them in the filing box," she said. "I know that the boys will enjoy the travel and animal stories very much. You always have such excellent reading matter here, and I am glad that you have returned so that your rental library is once more open. But now we must go, for I can see that Harold, now that he is acquainted with you, would ask questions all day if he were allowed to do so."

"Let the boys run over often," laughed George, smiling at them. "Next time I will tell Harold about the hunting dogs—real Russian wolfhounds that dad used to keep here on the place—and how they chased and killed the coyotes that were destroying the livestock for miles around."

"Oh, good," said Harold, joyfully clapping his hands. "I'll come again as soon as I can. And thank you for telling me such an interesting story today."

"Before you go, be sure to sign in the guest book. You see, that way I know how many callers I have each year."

"Do you have very many, away off here in this small town?" questioned the visitor.

"Indeed I do. Last year I had over seven thousand visitors, and that did not include my brothers and sisters and nieces and nephews who come almost every day."

Harold was silent on the way home, scuffing along with head bent downward. But he listened carefully to his Aunt Jessie.

"I am glad that you enjoyed your visit so much.

Everyone does. I often go over, especially when I feel that I need cheering, for George is always pleasant. He never complains or makes others feel sad for him. And he always has something interesting to talk about. His father used to take the children on camping trips into the woods with him, and so George grew up to be a real nature lover.

"Since his accident he has read a great deal, too, and he can answer almost any question on any subject that you care to question him about. It is no wonder that everyone loves him."

Harold was very quiet all evening. Even when bedtime came, he was still silent and went to bed without grumbling—the first time he had done so since his arrival.

John could scarcely believe his eyes when he saw his cousin's smiling face the next morning. Could this be the same sleepyhead who had to be coaxed and coaxed to get up, and who had whined and scowled and pouted for seven long days?

"Wake up," Harold grinned. "Let's eat breakfast and then go outside and do that weeding Aunt Jessie was talking about."

"Weeding!" gasped John. "But you said you hated weeding."

"I know I did, and I still do," answered Harold. "But I've been thinking that if George Hibbard, who can't even move his arms and legs, can run a library, and answer the telephone, and read and tell all kinds of stories, and make everybody like him and want to visit with him—" he paused for breath— "Well, if George can do all that when he's in bed all the time, I ought to be able to do something for somebody else, too. Especially when I can walk and run and jump and use my arms. So hurry up and get dressed. I'm going to work."

And he did, to the great surprise of everyone but wise Aunt Jessie. She knew what she was doing when she took her cross and complaining nephew to visit George Hibbard. And she was not surprised when he became a daily visitor to the Hibbard home.

But his father and mother *were* surprised when at the end of vacation time they came and found such a rosy-cheeked, happy, and truly helpful little son waiting for them.

8

King and Queen Go Hunting

"YOU'LL ENJOY that new book of dog stories," George Hibbard said. "And it has some very fine illustrations, too."

Harold looked up from his page-turning and smiled at the happy-faced librarian who lay helpless in bed.

"Yes, I just saw the picture of a big wolfhound." He leaned forward eagerly. "And that reminds me. The very first time that I came over here, you told me how you were paralyzed from the neck down in a diving accident; then, later on, you promised to tell me the story of the Russian wolfhounds. Would you have time today?"

George glanced at the mantel clock. "Well, let's see. It is almost two. Yes, I'll be able to tell one story before Dick comes for me. He's taking me down to the barbershop for a haircut and a shave."

He chuckled at the youngster's astonished look. "Perhaps you didn't know that I do more traveling than many people who have no injuries. It is possible for me to sit up in a large chair or a car seat for many hours at a time, if my body is properly braced. Why, only a few months ago I rode for twenty-six hours from here to Los Angeles." He stopped a moment.

"But I'll tell you of that trip some other time. Right now you shall hear about the imported Russian wolfhounds and the short-haired greyhounds that my father obtained through a famous Indian scout."

"Were they right here at your place?" quickly asked the visitor.

"Oh, yes. All this happened before I was born, but I have heard the story so often that it is very real to me. But first I'll ask you a question, Harold. Do you know anything about either the wolfhound or the greyhound?"

"N-no, I don't think so," slowly answered the interested boy. "I guess I've read the names, but that is all."

"Well," George continued, "the greyhound has long been called the dog of kings, and for hundreds of years it was possible for only noblemen to own that breed. It is believed by many that the greyhound is the oldest purebred dog in the world. Students of Egyptian history have found carvings on a tomb in the Nile Valley, engraved there thousands of years ago, showing dogs of the greyhound type. This is one of the wisest of the dog family, and is by nature very gentle.

"Now there are two types of hunting dogs: one type has a keen sense of smell, while the other depends more upon eyesight and speed. The greyhound belongs to this second class. He locates the hunted animal by his sharp eyesight and then overtakes his quarry by his great speed. With his short hair he can easily get through the brush."

"And what about the other dogs?" asked Harold, edging forward on his chair.

"The Russian wolfhound is also very swift and is a fine hunting dog on the plains.

"Dad owned purebred dogs of both types, and then he also crossbred them. He kept them here on the hill slope, safe within a large fenced-in enclosure, where they had enough space to exercise properly."

"How did they get their food? Did your father let them go out and hunt rabbits?"

"Oh, no," George laughed. "When the farmers lost any stock they would bring the dead animals in here

to be used for dog food. And bran was also part of their diet. My brother used to stick his face down in the barrel and then let the hounds lick off the bran. Of course he had to come into the house afterward and wash with soap and water.

"King and Queen were among dad's prize hunters. He used them for running down coyotes."

"Running down *what?*" blurted out Harold, forgetting in his excitement to ask pardon for his interruptions.

"Coyotes. I had forgotten that you have no doubt never seen one. However, you'll probably hear their shrill yapping bark and howl some moonlight night, for at times they come down close to the rimrock hills near town. The coyote is somewhat like the wolf, but he is smaller in build. He has a light gray-brown coat of fur that blends in perfectly with the gray sagebrush that covers the desert, and a hunter can pass within a few feet of his hiding place and not even see him lurking there.

"But not so with King and Queen. Oh, what champion hunters they were! When dad rode out, all ready for the hunt, they would joyfully bark, and then off they would go, far out across the valley until they reached the section where these beasts had destroyed livestock.

"Dad would stop and look carefully about. When he sighted a coyote he would call out, 'Here, King.' King would bound to his side, rear up on his saddle leg and gaze in the direction toward which his master pointed. His sharp eyesight always quickly spotted the hunted animal. With a leap King would spring away, leading the pack.   Then he would cut around the brush or fence, as he had been trained to do."

George ceased talking and laughed heartily.

"What in the world is so funny?" puzzled Harold.

"I just remember that dad once told me how King lost his tail.   He was in such a hurry to zip under a low fence that he caught his tail on a barbed wire.   The long tail broke and had to be docked.   Dad said that King had an almost human look of dismay at the accident."

"But did he catch the coyote?" urged the listener.

"When the well-trained dog pack gave full chase, a coyote had very little chance to escape, you may be sure, for a coyote cannot run very long at top speed.

"As soon as it was at bay and downed by the hounds, dad would quickly order them back and pick up the animal by the hind legs.   He then swung it overhead and broke the creature's neck on the ground.   The older method was to use a buggy spoke and, by hitting its head, put it to death with one swift blow.   However, this caused a blood clot on the pelt, lessening its sale value.   You see, there was a price paid for every skin, as the coyotes killed many valuable smaller animals, such as calves and lambs, and the ranchers were anxious to protect their stock.   One morning dad's hunting dogs finished eleven coyotes.

"Now coyotes are hunted by airplane and many of them are killed daily, but for hunting with dogs I believe that eleven is a very good record for one morning's hunt."

George ceased speaking as he again looked at the clock.   "But I must stop, for I hear Dick's car in the driveway right now. Do come again, Harold. I am always glad to see you and to tell you stories. You are a very interested listener."

"Why shouldn't I be, Mr. Hibbard?" replied Harold earnestly. "Thank you so much. You tell the best stories that I ever heard, and they are really true, too. Since hearing you, I don't care about made-up books at all."

"That's fine," George said. "You'll find that nature's truths are always far more interesting than man's fiction. I'm certainly glad to know that you have learned this valuable lesson."

9
Flashing Fangs

AS HAROLD entered the barber shop he stopped short in stunned surprise.

"Why, hello, Mr. Hibbard," he stammered, staring first at the shiny metal wheel chair and then at the happy face of its invalid occupant.

"Well, I'm certainly surprised to see you downtown," he hurriedly added. "But it's wonderful that you can get out this way. And your chair—when did you get it? And where——"

"Here, here," laughed George Hibbard, as he bent his head forward so that the barber could run the clippers over his strong, sunburned neck. "Not so fast, my young friend. I'll gladly answer your questions, but first I'm going to ask a few. Aren't you getting to be a regular summer visitor in Burns? Let me see; isn't this your third summer in eastern Oregon? Why, I believe that you really like our little town of Burns."

"Oh, I do," stoutly agreed Harold. "I like the boys

and girls and the people—they're so friendly. And I especially like you, Mr. Hibbard. You're always so pleasant and so much fun that I never think about your being paral——Well, I mean——" His voice trailed off as he stopped in confusion.

"That's quite all right, Harold. You needn't be embarrassed because you mentioned my paralyzed condition. Soon after my accident a number of years ago I made up my mind that if I lived I would never let people feel that I was essentially any different from anyone else. I've been fortunate, too, for though I am paralyzed from my neck down I still have full control of my voice, my hearing, and my eyesight. Thus there are many things that I can enjoy.

"But here, if you have time for a visit now, perhaps you'd like to push my chair up the hill to my home. I'll show you the motto of a famous group of people who are handicapped in everything but bravery of spirit, and then we'll talk awhile. I'll leave word here for Gene, my nephew, as he was coming back soon to take me home."

George Hibbard served as a rental librarian for the little Oregon city. As they entered his large, book-filled library bedroom, which overlooked the vast expanse of Harney Valley, he nodded his head toward a hand-lettered motto that hung near his bed.

"Read it aloud if you care to, Harold," he said quietly. "It has been a constant inspiration to me, as I am sure that it has been to countless others."

"Never Martyrdom shall I seek;
Never Sarcasm shall I speak;
Never Ingratitude shall I show;

Never Discontented shall I grow;
Never Sympathy shall I desire;
Never Self-pity shall I acquire.

"Never Unhappiness shall I spread;
Never Tears of Remorse shall I shed;
Never Sorrow shall I sing;
Never to Selfishness shall I cling;
Never Criticism shall I write;
Never of God shall I lose sight."

Harold's voice stopped, and he drew a deep breath before he again spoke. "Why, that's a wonderful poem," he volunteered soberly. "And you're just like that, too, Mr. Hibbard."

"Thank you, Harold, I'm afraid I'm not like that, although I try to be," the librarian said quietly. "But here. Do you remember the long, rubber-tipped stick which I hold in my mouth when reading and with which I turn the pages of the book or magazine? Yes, I see that you do. Then you'll be interested in knowing that I've found a further use for that trusty stick and for my good strong teeth. Can you guess what it is?"

"Another use?" Puzzled, the youthful visitor wrinkled his forehead and shook his head. "N-n-no, I can't imagine."

"Well, quite soon I expect to have my new electric typewriter, and as soon as it comes I'll invite you over to watch me use it," stated George.

"Use a typewriter!" gasped Harold, sitting suddenly forward on his chair. "But—but how, when you can't move your arms at all, and——"

"Didn't I tell you that I'd found a further use for my trusty stick?" queried George, laughing heartily at Harold's amazement.

"You mean you type with *that?*" the boy blurted out.

"Correct! While visiting my sisters in Portland last summer I had an opportunity to use a borrowed electric typewriter. I sat up in my new wheel chair, held this rubber-tipped stick in my mouth, lightly touched it to the keys, and wrote for six hours the first day. When I finished I was exhausted, but happier by far than I had been for years."

"Why, that's wonderful!" exclaimed Harold. "But how did you ever get the idea of trying to do this? I'd never have known enough to even try."

"A friend of mine who had attended a writers' conference told me that there she had met an extremely talented crippled girl who had the use of just one finger for typing. She said that she was sure that I could do as well, and to my surprise I found that I really could type on one of these easily operated new machines. Certainly I shall be very happy when I own one."

"Are you going to write any stories, Mr. Hibbard?" eagerly questioned Harold. "Last summer you said that you'd like to put down on paper some of your experiences. I think that the stories you've told me would make exciting reading for any boy or girl. I've never forgotten 'King and Queen Go Hunting,' or the snake story, 'Double Death.' I've told them ever so many times."

"Yes, Harold, that's just what I hope to do," nodded George. "I don't know about stories, but I'm going to try some nature articles. Whatever I write will be true, however, for I don't care to waste my time writing fiction. There are too many wonderful wildlife stories just waiting to be told."

"I know that," solemnly agreed the visitor. "Do you remember that when I first met you I didn't know anything about the out-of-doors? Then you began telling me stories about snakes and deer and coyotes and——Why, that reminds me! In school last term our teacher read us a story about Louis Pasteur and his discovery of a cure for hydrophobia. Right away I thought about you, and wondered if you'd ever seen a mad dog or a mad coyote. None of us had—not even our teacher."

"Yes, Harold, as a matter of fact, I have," said George rather soberly. "And it is a fearful sight—one that I would not care to see again. Would you like to hear the story?"

"Oh, indeed I would," eagerly assented Harold, drawing his chair as close as possible to George's wheel chair. "Please tell me."

"Well, this happened a number of years ago, long before you were born. It was late in the fall. In fact, it lacked only a few weeks of being Christmas when that dreadful disease influenza began to strike down members of almost every Burns family.

"Today we speak of it as the flu. And today the patient calls his doctor, obtains one of the new miracle drugs, and recovers rapidly. But soon after World War I, when people in the United States first experienced a real influenza epidemic, to be ill with this disease was a matter of life or death. Many people died, for there were no miracle drugs then, and nurses were scarce. Mother became very much alarmed, and insisted that she be allowed to take all of us children out of town to our small mountain cabin.

" 'You'll have to stay here so that you can see as many of your dental patients as possible,' she told my father, 'and Roberta had better stay to cook for you. Every few days you can bring necessary supplies up as far as the pasture gate, and in that way we'll manage all right. I dare not expose the children to this epidemic. Several of them have had colds all fall and the influenza might prove fatal. I'm sure that it is best for us to go to the mountains.'

"After much discussion my father reluctantly agreed to this plan, and within a few days we had moved some miles out of town, up in the foothills of the Blue Mountains.

"By now the weather had turned very cold, and the older boys were kept busy chopping down small trees near the cabin, sawing and cutting them into stovewood lengths, and piling them in neat stacks against the outer cabin walls. Mother was determined to prepare for a real siege, if need be."

"Did you cut down any of the trees?" questioned Harold.

"Oh, no. I was very small then, but I felt that I was really doing most of the work when I went out and filled the chip basket with the fragments of wood and bark, which we used for kindling. You see, this was before our present days of automatic furnace heat and electric or gas ranges.

"It was also before the time of kitchen sinks and hot

and cold running water in the average home. We had the running water all right, but it was in an icy mountain creek several hundred yards away. I usually felt it my duty to go with the girls when they took the water buckets down to the willow-bordered stream to fill them and carry them back to the kitchen. Sometimes we had to crack the ice in order to dip those buckets into the creek."

"Br-r-r! That must have been cold work," broke in Harold. "It makes my teeth chatter just to think about it. All that work to get water! I guess I've never appreciated our water faucets as much as I should."

"You probably haven't," nodded the librarian. "We often don't appreciate the many conveniences that we now have until we realize that people lived—and many still do—without them.

"But I must hurry on with my story. I neglected to tell you that we took our young dog along with us when we left Burns. I guess that I was really responsible for including him in the family group. He was a fine sheep dog, and I had claimed him for my very own. During our waking hours we were inseparable, as we were during our sleeping hours, for nothing would do but that Shep must sleep on a clean gunny sack at the foot of my bed.

"Although at that time I was the baby of the family, mother never seemed the least bit nervous about having me outside, for Shep watched me with an eagle eye. And no small wild creature or stranger ever approached me without Shep barking a warning that all could hear.

"On this particular day dad had come up as far as the pasture gate and had brought food and other provisions for us, as well as local news of interest to mother. She had gone down to meet and talk with him, for he did not want to come near us children, thinking that from contact with his patients he might carry upon him the dread influenza germs. I can remember that she looked very sober-faced as she returned to the cabin, calling to the older boys to carry up the supplies and put them in the kitchen. But it was not until evening that she told us this news.

" 'Children,' she said, as we stood around the glowing, pot-bellied stove, 'your father told me that another terrible disease has broken out in Harney County.' "

"But what *could* be worse?" anxiously asked the young listener. "Didn't you say that the influenza epidemic killed a number of people?"

"Yes, Harold, it did," nodded George, "but this other disease was the dreaded and terrible one that until a few years ago doomed its hundreds of victims to a certain, horrible end. This disease was called rabies, or hydrophobia."

"Oo-h!" exclaimed the boy. "Now I understand. And it wasn't until Louis Pasteur found a serum for the bite of a mad animal that anyone attacked could hope to be saved. What an awful thing that must have been—to have had no hope of a cure."

"That is the very thing my mother mentioned that evening as she told us my father's message. She warned us to be very careful to stay near the house. She told us we must not wander outside the fence except on necessary errands, and in that case the older boys would go armed. Dad had told her that many rabid coyotes were running rampant through the fields and mountains, biting anything unfortunate enough to cross their paths. One of dad's friends had narrowly escaped a sudden attack by his prize bull, which had suddenly gone mad.

"Well, for a few days I was afraid to go outdoors. We kept Shep cooped up inside with us, too, but at last the dog became so restless that we mustered up enough courage to go out near the back porch. Nothing occurred to frighten any of us, and as we saw no signs of any wild animals near the ranch, we gradually became bolder and bolder. It was not long before I completely forgot about any possible danger.

"On this particular early evening I had gone to the creek with Eugenia and Hazel, but when they started back to the house with the heavy, dripping water bucket sagging between them, I stayed by the water's edge. Shep had spied a big gray jack rabbit and had started off in fast pursuit. By the time I had called and whistled him back to my side the girls had entered the house, so I decided to wander just a few steps farther along the creek bank.

"We walked farther than I had intended, when suddenly a low growl from Shep abruptly halted me.

" 'What is it, boy?' I called. 'Come on, Shep. That rabbit's far away over the hills by this time. Stop your growling and come along.' Another louder growl from Shep was my answer. I looked intently at him and felt my heart beat faster as I noticed his stiff-legged pose and saw him bare his long white teeth. His brown eyes glared fiercely toward the woods which crowded down close to our small barn, and the hairs on the back of his neck fairly bristled.

" 'Come on, old boy. Come here,' I again commanded. But Shep paid no attention to me.

"A sound caught my ears and I stopped dead still as the crashing noise of breaking bushes and tree branches echoed and re-echoed through the hills. Nearer and nearer it came, and Shep's growls increased in fierceness and in volume.

" 'What can it be?' I thought desperately. 'A hungry bear? A cougar?' Even then the true explanation did not occur to me until all at once a rough, gray-furred animal staggered out of the willows. It bumped blindly against first one tree and then another, but still plunged onward in its mad flight. Straight toward me it came, red eyes gleaming, hanging jaws covered with froth.

"I was absolutely frozen with fear. For the moment I couldn't have moved if my life had depended upon it. I stood there for what seemed an eternity, while larger and larger loomed the rabid animal. And then, just as Shep leaped forward, I heard my mother scream.

" 'Run, George. Run for your life.'

"Her piercing cry broke through my spellbound fright so that just as Shep sprang at the raging coyote I turned and fled, sobbing with fright.

"Though I ran faster and faster, the cabin seemed to move farther and farther away, until I despaired of ever reaching its safety. But reach home I did, to collapse into my mother's waiting arms. Quickly she pulled me inside and bolted the door.

"Mother and all of us children huddled together while the fight raged outside. It was dreadful to listen to the snarls and growls of the brave dog and the mad coyote, and to feel the thud of their bodies as, time after time, they crashed against the cabin walls.

"At last it was all over. Now the only sound outside was the rippling of the swift mountain stream as it rushed downhill and the faint, faraway eerie bark of a distant coyote.

" 'I'm going out, Mother. I'm going out there to get Shep,' I wailed, as I raised my swollen, tear-stained face from mother's lap.

" 'Wait, dear,' she counseled. 'Wait awhile until we're sure it's safe to go.'

"To the loud tick-tock of the old clock the minutes dragged slowly by. At last mother rose and crossed the room to the kitchen door. She reached up to the deerhorn wall rack and took down dad's old gun.

" 'I want all of you to stay in this room,' she said. 'Yes, you older children as well. I'm going to step out on the porch and look for Shep, but none of you are to come unless I call for you. Do you understand?'

"The older children nodded solemnly and I choked out a tearful 'Yes, Mother,' for I was just a small boy, and Shep was my dearest treasure.

"It seemed as though a long, long time passed by, but I suppose that in reality it was but a moment or so. And then—we heard a shot. Just one shot! I screamed and clutched Eugenia, while the boys, forgetful of mother's orders, ran outside."

"What—what had happened?" stammered Harold breathlessly.

"A very wonderful and heart-touching thing had occurred," gravely answered George. "When mother

stepped out onto the back porch, the gun aimed at whatever danger might be in her way, she saw a sight that
brought tears to her eyes. There, near the back steps,
mangled and dead, lay the body of the mad coyote, and
halfway up the stairway, where he had crawled in his
frantic desire to reach us, lay poor Shep, unconscious
and bleeding.

"Mother has often said that she had never performed
any harder task than that which she had to do at that
time. Taking careful aim, she——"

"Shot Shep? Your mother shot the dog that had saved
your life? Oh, how could she! That was cruel," exclaimed
Harold, with tears in his own eyes.

"I know how you feel, Harold," nodded George, "for
I was heartbroken when she told me. It was a long time
before I really recovered from my grief, but now I understand that what mother did was the kindest service that
she could have performed for Shep. He was so badly
injured that he could not have lived, and even if he had
lived, he would have developed hydrophobia, for the
coyote was mad."

"But couldn't Shep have been given the Pasteur treatment? Couldn't something have been done for him?" pro-
tested Harold.

"You must remember that we were miles from town,
without telephone service and without transportation.
And then it was a long and expensive journey from Burns
to a large city where such a treatment at that time might
have been available. There were a number of good rea-
sons why mother's brave action was the only logical one,
hard though it seemed to us then.

"But Shep had a funeral—what we called a military funeral—for we fired a gun salute over his grave. Then we made a wooden tombstone and carved his name deeply upon it. The weather-beaten letters are there to this day:

SHEP

A BRAVE DOG

HE DIED TO SAVE OTHERS

"After this event we did not remain very long at the cabin, for mother was afraid that other rabid animals might come near. As soon as dad made his next trip up to see us, we returned to town with him. Before we left, I cried again over Shep's grave and vowed that I would never forget him. And I never have, for he was in truth a noble creature and one who gladly laid down his life for his friends.

"But, there, Harold, I'm afraid this story has been a sad one, and I don't want you to think that all our summer visits will bring tears to your eyes. Come over again soon, and I'll tell you about the nest of gold that Eugenia found in the rimrock."

"I surely will, Mr. Hibbard. And while your other stories may be more cheerful than this one, they surely can't be any more thrilling," said Harold. "My school friends will certainly sit up and take notice when I tell them your story of the 'Flashing Fangs.' "

10
Desert Capture

"COME IN, Harold," called George Hibbard, as Harold knocked at the half-opened door. "I was just hoping that you'd come over this morning. I want you to meet Margaret Ann Williamson, and then you can listen to the story that I've promised to tell her. Margaret Ann's mother lived here in Burns when she was a little girl. She used to spend a great deal of time right here in our yard, playing with my brothers and sisters. Now Margaret Ann is visiting her cousin, Sally Donegan. She's been begging me for an animal story, so now that you're here I'll have an audience of two listeners."

Harold smiled at the little blue-eyed girl who sat so primly in the leather chair by the librarian's bed, and she smiled shyly in return.

"What's the story today, Mr. Hibbard?" the boy questioned eagerly. "I do hope it's about the nest of gold that you mentioned last time. I've been looking forward to hearing that one ever since then. It sounds quite mysterious."

"No, we'll wait until next time for the story of the nest. Margaret Ann's especially interested in horses, and so I'm going to tell her about an animal that can outrun the swiftest horse. In fact, it can outdistance most land animals, even when painfully wounded. It has been known to travel sixty miles an hour."

"Then it must be a coyote," broke in Margaret Ann, her eyes glistening with excitement. "We saw one out on the desert between here and Bend."

"No, it isn't a coyote," answered George, shaking his head. "This animal is the American pronghorn antelope, which is found only in North America. Before I tell you the story, which I first heard from my father, I'll tell you young people a little about the antelope.

"Many years ago there were millions of antelopes in the West, where they, like the buffalo, provided food for the Indians. Then, as the white man began to hunt with guns, these huge herds were almost wiped out. In addition, many of those surviving fell prey to a cattle disease called fossy-jaw. Finally, about 1900, only a few of these interesting animals remained, and they were found only in the most isolated parts of the country.

"About 1910 various wildlife enthusiasts laid plans to preserve this game animal. In 1924 there were less than 26,000 of them left in the United States, but since then refuges have been established by the Government in Nevada, Wyoming, and Oregon, and in 1937 the number had increased to 130,000."

"Did you say that there was an antelope refuge in Oregon?" inquired Harold. "I've never heard that before. Where is it, or do you know?"

"Indeed I do," smiled George. "The Hart Mountain Antelope Refuge is located in near-by Lake County, in the midst of strange mountains formed of dark, volcanic rock. There the protected animals have increased from only 200 to many thousands. Perhaps someday you can go there, for it is a very interesting place.

"But I must hurry on with my story. It is in May or early June that the female gives birth to two or three fawns. The mother cunningly hides them for the first two days, but by the end of that short time the fawns are swift runners, and within a month they are able to equal the speed of their parents. In fact, it is this speed which often saves the animal from death, although if necessary a mother will turn and fight with her sharp hoofs to defend her fawns.

"Some years ago my father started for the mountains for the express purpose of trying to find and capture a young antelope. As a member of the game commission he felt it necessary to know as much about wildlife as possible. Since it is almost impossible to get near the antelope in his natural surroundings, it was dad's intention to bring a young animal here, where it could live in safety in the enclosed pasture adjoining our place, and from which location he could easily study and observe its actions.

"When dad reached a small, rimrock-enclosed valley he tied his horse behind a tree and then cautiously crept up on a large rock, where he lay flat, looking out through his field glasses."

"Oh, what did he see?" breathed Margaret Ann, holding her hands tightly together.

"What do you think he saw, Harold?" smiled George,

looking from one interested young face to the other.

"An antelope?" replied Harold.

"Yes, he saw an old mother antelope running nervously about whenever any moving thing came into the valley, which she considered her special property. Even swooping eagles and preying hawks were driven away as she charged at them. In addition to this, dad saw the flaring white rosette, formed by the white hairs on the animal's rump. These hairs are raised whenever the animal is alarmed, and they show up plainly even though its tan coat cannot be seen among the sagebrush and rocks.

"Dad knew then that the fawns must be somewhere in that little valley. He knew, also, that if he could only wait patiently he might be lucky enough to see them, for the antelope mother nurses her young ones every two hours. She will feed near them, and then when it is time for them to nurse, she will go toward their hiding place and give some kind of signal."

"What does she do, Mr. Hibbard?" broke in Harold, quite forgetting his accustomed politeness in his interest in the story. "Does she call out?"

"No one has ever been able to learn what signal is given," replied George, "but the young ones come out at once from their hiding place, nurse for about five minutes, and walk about at the mother's heels for exercise. Then the mother antelope, without turning her head or making any audible sound, gives the same mysterious signal. The fawns turn at right angles and go off about 50 or 75 steps into the sage brush, where they hide themselves so well that if you were to pass within several feet of them you probably would not see them."

"Did your father get to see the little babies?" burst forth Margaret Ann, eager to know the answer right away.

"Dad said that he lay on that hard rock for twelve long hours, from six o'clock in the morning to six o'clock at night, but not once did he see that mother nurse her little ones. He didn't know whether she sensed his presence there or what had happened, but he was sure there was some unusual reason for her apparent neglect.

"And then, late in the afternoon, just when dad was about ready to give up and start for home, he saw the mother swerve near a juniper tree. Just as she reached it, a large bobcat jumped down from the branches and ran full speed for the safety of the rimrock some distance away.

"Dad was astonished to see the mother antelope leap in pursuit of the fleeing bobcat. Because of her great speed she soon caught up with the killer. With one bound she struck him with her shoulder, sending the bobcat sprawling into the near-by brush. Hurriedly he struggled to his feet and again started running for safety. Again she struck him with her shoulder, and again he

sprawled flat upon the ground. This happened several times, but at last the frightened bobcat reached the rim-rock and disappeared from sight. I imagine that had he not jumped hastily to his feet each time, she would have trampled him to death beneath her sharp hoofs."

"And did your father get to see the baby fawns?" asked Margaret Ann, cheeks red with excitement. "Oh, I hope he did."

"Yes," nodded George, "he really saw the babies, for after the treed bobcat left the little valley, the mother became less and less nervous. Finally her fluff went down, and soon she gave the signal for the little ones to come out of hiding and nurse. How hungry those poor babies must have been all day, but not once had they dared to show their little noses without hearing their mother's command to come out from hiding.

"Dad carefully marked the spot where they went into hiding, and after the mother had wandered some distance away, he ran down the slope into the valley, cornered one of the fawns, and brought it home, where it became a family pet."

"Oh, it seems cruel to take away her fawn," exclaimed Harold, "especially when she was so brave and had worked so hard to save the little fellows from the bobcat."

"It might seem that way," agreed George, "unless you remember why dad wanted to capture a small antelope. The mother still had her other babies, and dad had the young animal, which he could observe and study. Fluffy never lacked for care and attention, you may be sure.

"You would have laughed if you could have seen him with his foster mother, Nanny, one of our best milk goats. They became very good friends, although when Fluffy was only four months old he was as large as Nanny. Fluffy had the run of the place and would even frolic along near-by streets, much to the delight of all the neighborhood children. But when mealtime rolled around, he was right back here with Nanny, and whenever dad came home, the little fellow followed him about just like a puppy. Why, he used to come right in here to see me, and I wish you could have seen the expression on his antelope face when he first walked across the slick linoleum. He looked so comical, just as though he'd like to say, 'My, my, what queer-feeling dirt you have in here! I can barely stand up!'

"And that ends the true story of Fluffy, an American pronghorn antelope who lived right here in the Hibbard yard," smiled George.

"Oh, I just loved that story," sighed Margaret Ann. "I wish you'd tell us another one. Won't you, please?"

"Yes, that surely was interesting, Mr. Hibbard," agreed Harold. "Now I've learned something else which I can pass along to my nature class at school. Thanks very much."

"You're both welcome," said George pleasantly. "But I think I'll have to beg off for today. A friend is coming by to take me for a ride, and I must get ready. But if you will come over again soon I'll be glad to visit with you."

"Good-by, and thank you again," Margaret Ann and Harold said as they went out the door. Harold called back, "And I'll be waiting to hear about the nest of gold."

11

Terror on the Trestle

I'M SICK and tired of carrying all these clanking pots and pans around all over the country. Why can't Willie help out a little! Every morning after we have breakfast and put out our campfire, he finds some excuse for going on ahead." Harry glowered down at the rough seaside trail and wished for the hundredth time that he were an older brother who could do as he pleased.

"I'm tired too," moaned Ralph, shifting the big bedding roll over to the middle of his bicycle rack. "Just look at all the things my brother makes me carry. Why in the world did we buy all this food, anyway! We'll never be able to eat so much. Well, just you wait—some of these days I'll be as big as Willie, and then I'll let him carry his own things. Just see if I don't." He looked toward the third member of the group in time to see him nod in decided agreement.

Sunk in their gloomy self-pity, the three young boys, Jesse, Ralph, and Harry plodded sullenly along the future

Coastal Highway roadbed, blind to the breathtaking beauty of the rolling Pacific Ocean spread far out below them.

It had been about a week since the group had left their homes in Eugene and had started on the long-anticipated trip to the coast. There they planned to meet their friend Roy, whose father was owner of a large construction camp. Willie and Roy, who were older, had planned the excursion, and they had received many instructions from the fathers of the younger boys. For the first two or three days all had gone well, until the newness of their unaccustomed freedom had worn off. Then Willie had begun to travel with less and less equipment, and the three younger boys, much to their surprise, with more and more.

"We surely ought to reach that construction camp tonight," Jesse broke in. "Won't I be glad to get there and eat some of the cook's meals for a change! After a few breakfasts of Willie's pancakes I could eat shoe leather and call it good. Whoever told him that he could cook?"

Harry and Ralph grinned, in spite of their depression, and pushed their dusty bicycles forward a little faster.

"We're going to have to hurry if we catch up with him," puffed Ralph, as they guided their wheels up and down hill. "I want to get to camp as soon as he does, and then we'll have a chance to pick out our own bunks and not take what Willie and Roy think we should have. For once I'd like to get something besides the leftovers."

An hour or two went by, but still there was no sight of the older boy.

"Whew!" gasped Ralph, as they reached the summit

of a steep hill. "I'm going to have to sit down here awhile and rest. I'm all tired out."

"Oh, come on," urged Jesse, his dark hair ruffling in the stiff ocean breeze. "It can't be far now. Why, look down there! See? There's the railroad trestle that's being built. It's surely a long one. We'll have to cross it to get to the other side. The construction camp isn't very far away from there, I'm sure."

"Cross that?" asked Harry in amazement. "How are we going to wheel these loaded bikes across those bumpy ties? There's nothing else there except the steel rails and those little water barrel platforms sticking out along the side every few yards. Excuse me, but I'll get there some other way."

"How?" inquired practical Jesse. "There isn't any other way. That's the only road so far, so we'll either have to cross it, or go back home, and I for one am not going back home now." He stood up and lifted his bicycle with its load of clattering kettles. "Are you coming with me?"

"Pretty soon," groaned Ralph, rubbing his aching legs and tightening the buckles of his knee pants. "Harry and I will come along in a little while. I've got to rest first, though." He turned to his doubting friend, "We can make it all right, Harry. No trains'll be running yet over this new road. If we take our time, we'll get across safe and sound. Go ahead, Jesse. We'll catch up with you."

Slowly but surely Jesse inched his way across the huge, open railroad trestle, wheeling his bike carefully beside the shining steel rails. It made him dizzy to look down through the four-inch spaces between the ties and see the lapping waves far, far below. He was glad to rest

at frequent intervals beside the tiny platforms that jutted out from the side of the rails. There was barely room for him to stand next to the water barrel and hold on to its edge to steady himself, but he was glad for even this chance of grasping a solid support.

At last he stepped off the narrow trestle. He heaved a deep sigh of relief as he turned and looked back over the quarter-mile crossing.

"Say, but I'm glad that's over," he muttered to himself. "I'd hate to go through that experience again. I'm still dizzy from walking between those rails."

He took out a crumpled red bandanna handkerchief and mopped his flushed face. As he restored it to his pocket he saw the faraway figures of Ralph and Harry just stepping out on the beginning of their perilous journey.

"Oh, oh," he thought sympathetically, "here they come. Look at Harry wobble along. He'd better be careful, or he'll fall off. What a splash *that* would make." He shivered as he eyed the great distance from the narrow trestle to the ocean inlet below. "Maybe I'd better leave my things here and go back to help him. Ralph'll make it—he's used to climbing tall trees, and he doesn't get dizzy—but Harry's scared. I can tell that!"

Jesse leaned his wheel against a tall clump of golden Scotchbroom and started back toward his friends. He had walked about a block when he first heard the faraway sound.

"Ooooooo-ooo. Ooooooooo-oooo," it echoed mournfully.

Again the startled boy heard the mournful wail.

"Ooooooo-ooo. Oooooooooo-oooo!"

"Get off the track!" it seemed to shriek. "Get off the track. I'm c-o-o-o-o-o-ming! I'm c-o-o-o-o-o-ming!"

"The train!" Jesse yelled to Ralph and Harry, who were now exactly halfway across the bridge. "The train's coming. Drop your bikes. Run for your lives."

Then he turned and ran back to his bicycle beside the Scotchbroom. As he hurled himself off the trestle he heard the clattering of the train wheels around the bend.

"They'll never make it," Jesse gasped. He cupped his hands around his mouth and yelled with all his strength.

"Drop your bikes over the edge. Drop them, I say. And run. Run!"

Louder and louder roared the onrushing train. With another earsplitting shriek the great engine rushed into sight and started toward the trestle. Bells clanged as the engineer waved wildly at the boys to save themselves.

Jesse could not turn his horrified look from Ralph and Harry. He could not speak. He could not call out. All he could do was to stand, terrified, to watch his best friends fall beneath the grinding wheels of the monster. And then his heart gave a leap as his eyes fell upon the small water barrel platforms that had afforded welcome resting places during his crossing. It was a chance in a million, but it might work.

"Get on the platform!" he screamed, jumping up and down and pointing toward the nearest one. "*Get on the platform!*" His words were drowned in the great rush of the approaching gravel train, but his gestures could be seen and understood. And Ralph, stumbling desperately ahead of Harry, understood Jesse's frantic motions.

Jesse's frightened eyes saw Ralph lurch forward in one great jump. He saw him grasp the water barrel with one hand while he clutched his bicycle with the other, pulling and tugging until it hung over the edge beside him. There it swayed back and forth, high above the rolling tide far below. And just at that instant the train thundered by, sparks flying from beneath the wheels, smoke belching from the smokestack. On, on, the iron wheels hurtled, flashing past Ralph and toward Harry.

But just then Jesse saw that Harry, too, now clung to the safety of another water barrel and that his bicycle also dangled far out over the platform's edge.

Weak with relief, Jesse watched the shaking, trembling boys inch their way across the intervening space. As soon as they reached the road they fell flat upon the ground, and there they lay for some time.

"Was that a narrow escape!" Jesse blurted, when he had regained his breath. "I was never so scared as when I heard that train whistle."

"Scared!" exclaimed Ralph. "My knees were nothing but jelly. I don't know how in the world I ever got out onto that platform."

"Me, either," wheezed Harry. "All I can remember is seeing that train bearing down on me. Then somehow I saw you waving, Jesse, and all at once I was out on a platform, just like Ralph. Oh, but I was frightened!"

It was some time before the three youthful adventurers felt strong enough to continue the short remaining distance to the camp. But at length they arrived there, to be greeted by Roy, his father, and the camp cook—who listened with interest to their exciting adventure.

In the following hours, as they became the center of attention for the returning work crews, they quite forgot their early morning grievance toward Willie and Roy. In fact, they almost felt sorry for the two older boys, who were completely unnoticed and in the background during the entire evening while the men complimented the boys on their quick thinking.

"Maybe it's a good thing to be a younger brother sometimes," grinned Jesse early that night, as he and Ralph and Harry curled up in the best bunks in the bunkhouse. "At least this is one time when being left behind with all the pots and pans and bedding proved to be exciting."

"That may be," agreed Harry, "but as far as I'm concerned you can have all the railroad trestles you want. I wouldn't go through that experience again for a million dollars. I'll gladly leave my share of all those supplies right here for the camp rather than carry them back across that trestle. I told you we'd never be able to use all that food we brought along. We certainly don't need it here, where all our meals are furnished."

"Well, cheer up," grinned Ralph. "We can take our supplies back with us and use them when we go camping up the McKenzie River. Our good friend the cook said that he could arrange for us to ride back to Eugene in the gravel train. That'll be a lot easier than bicycling 125 miles. Won't it be fun to load everything into the caboose and then just sit back and rest?"

"Three cheers!" shouted Jesse. "Three cheers for the cook and the gravel train."

12

Fire in the Night

Darlene, will you please answer the telephone for me? I'm busy right now," called mother from the kitchen. "See who it is, and tell them I'll be right there."

Darlene put down the handful of silverware with which she was setting the table and hurriedly picked up the receiver.

"Hello. Oh, yes, Mrs. Thompson. Why, I think I could, but I'll have to ask mother first. May I call you in a few minutes, or do you want to wait while I find out? All right, I'll let you know right away."

Darlene hung up the receiver and rushed into the kitchen, her eyes shining with delight. "Mother, guess what Mrs. Thompson wants! Just guess! No, let me tell you instead. She wants me—ME—to come over this evening and stay with the children while she and Mr. Thompson go out. She said that Evelyn had a cold and couldn't be there, and so she thought she'd call me. Now I'll get to help put the baby to bed and tell Judy a good-night story. Please let me go, Mother. We've been over there visiting so many times that I'm sure I'll know just what to do."

She watched breathlessly until mother spoke; then her face clouded with disappointment at the answer.

"I'm sorry, dear, but I'd rather not let you go. It's a school night, and you need your ten hours' sleep. The Thompsons don't have a free evening very often, and I imagine that they'll stay out rather late. This would mean that you would have to stay awake, for you sleep so soundly that you'd never hear the children if you went to bed. You're only eleven; when you are older, there'll be plenty of time for baby sitting. But it was nice of Mrs. Thompson to telephone. It shows that she has confidence in you and believes you to be trustworthy."

"But, Mother," wailed Darlene, "you just don't understand. They aren't going out for pleasure. Mr. Thompson's sister is quite sick and they have to go 'way over on the other side of town to see her and take some medicine and things that she needs. Mrs. Thompson said she wouldn't have asked me otherwise, because she knew I went to bed early."

"Well, that does put a different face on the matter," mother briskly replied. "I'll call Mrs. Thompson myself. If it's an emergency, we should do what we can to help."

At seven-thirty Darlene settled herself comfortably in a large rocker in the Thompson home and opened her new Junior Reading Course book. Two-year-old Judy and four-month-old Tony had been lovingly tucked in their cribs, and their parents had just left, promising to be back as soon as possible.

"I'm sure that you'll be warm, dear," Mrs. Thompson had said. "Dan stoked the new furnace about an hour ago, so you won't need to do a thing with the heating plant. The children sleep soundly; just look in their room a time or two to see that they are well covered. Other than that there is nothing for you to do but just be here. We'll leave Cookie; she's a good little watchdog and will keep you company until we return."

Although this was Darlene's first experience as nursemaid in sole charge, she found it a pleasant one. For an hour she read without interruption, and then stopped only because her eyes began to feel heavy.

"Eight-thirty!" she exclaimed to the red cocker spaniel, who for the past few minutes had been padding restlessly toward the door and back again. "It's eight-thirty already, and half-an-hour past my usual bedtime. No wonder I'm getting sleepy."

She rubbed her eyes with the back of one hand as she listened to the little click-click of Cookie's toenails on the hardwood floor.

"Oh, lie down, Cookie. What's wrong with you! You make me nervous when you prowl around that way. Lie down over here by me like a good dog. Come on."

But, coax as she would, Cookie would not lie down. Back and forth she walked, first toward one door and then toward another.

"I do believe you want me to go in and look at the children. Is that it?" Darlene spoke aloud, smiling down at the nervous little pet. "Come along with me, then. We'll see if Judy and Tony are covered up."

Together they quietly entered the bedroom to find

that all was well; the little tots were sound asleep and well covered. Darlene was amused at the way the cocker spaniel carefully sniffed at the bed covers and poked her black nose into each corner of the room.

Again Darlene settled herself in the big chair, but this time it was much harder to keep awake. In fact, several times she dozed and then sat up with a jerk that hurt her neck. At last she felt as though she couldn't stay awake another second. "I'll just close my eyes for one minute," she afterward recalled thinking. "It'll rest them after so much reading." And that was the last she knew until she heard Cookie's frantic bark and felt the dog's cold nose repeatedly nudging her hand.

"Bow-wow," barked Cookie. "Bow-wow-wow!" Over and over she signaled, dog fashion, running back and forth between Darlene and the closed door. The cocker's eyes were wide with excitement; she seemed to be doing her best to tell Darlene something of great importance.

Darlene's sleepy eyes just barely opened as she staggered drowsily to her feet. "What in the world is wrong with you, Cookie?" she asked almost crossly. "The children are all right. It hasn't been very long since we were in there to look at them."

As she spoke she looked at the clock. Instantly she was jolted wide awake. Eleven o'clock! Surely something must have happened to delay the Thompsons. Why, even on Saturday night she was seldom allowed to stay up until eleven o'clock, and on a school night it was an unheard-of event. What would mother say! Well, she knew that it meant that never again could she stay at the Thompsons as a baby sitter, although she could often come with mother to pay a friendly call and play with the babies. They were such darlings. How she loved to play with Judy and wheel little Tony out in the yard.

"Bow-wow-wow," again barked Cookie, looking desperately toward the door.

"All right, all right," Darlene said. "Come on. We'll go across the hall together."

She had no more than flung open the living room door than she knew the answer to Cookie's restlessness. For suddenly she smelled smoke. She could not tell from what direction it came, but it was unmistakably smoke.

"It must be from the new furnace that Mr. Thompson just put in," she thought, hurrying toward the nursery. "After I look at Judy and Tony I suppose I should go down to the furnace, but I wouldn't know what to do if anything was wrong. Oh, dear. I wish the folks would come home."

As her hand reached for the doorknob Cookie's barking rose to a loud crescendo. Instantly Darlene gasped and jerked away her fingers. A chill ran down her back as she stared at the door. She listened intently. What was that? Again she listened carefully. Then she heard it very distinctly—a tiny crackling noise that whitened her cheeks and started her knees trembling.

Without an instant's hesitation she grasped the knob and flung open the door. A burst of flame and smoke shot out into the hall. Darlene shrank back in horror. Cookie stood stanchly by her side, hair bristling, white teeth showing as she snarled.

"Oh, oh, the whole room's on fire," sobbed Darlene, wringing her hands. "What shall I do! The babies are in there. They'll be burned to death. And the fire's spreading—it'll burn the whole house down. Oh, what can I do!"

She started toward the doorway, only to be met with another burst of smoke and flame. She heard Tony's cough and Judy's answering cry. She must get them. She must! But how?

As she looked down at the frantic little dog she noticed for the first time the heavy handmade wool rug upon which she stood. "I wonder——" she thought. "If I put this over my head, could I get into the room? I mustn't breathe the smoke, or I'll die. But I must go in there and get them out now, or it'll be too late."

Instantly Darlene stooped and jerked up the new hall rug of which Mrs. Thompson was so proud. Quickly she threw it over her head and shoulders. She looked in the direction of the two little beds, side by side. And then, taking a deep breath, she plunged desperately into the terrific heat. Cookie ran by her side, barking loudly. At once Darlene smelled the singeing hair upon the little pet as Cookie brushed against a smoldering baseboard. Stooping, so as not to dislodge her covering, she grabbed Judy, who clung desperately around her neck. Then she snatched up limp little Tony and, guided by Cookie's barking, groped her way into the hall, which was even then beginning to blaze.

On and on the two little figures struggled through the fire and smoke. On and on, until at last they staggered across the porch and out onto the lawn, where Darlene fell in a heap, releasing her precious burden. As she flung off the charring rug and stamped on it, she heard the loud crash of the bedroom wall as it fell in upon the very spot where such a short time before two little babies had been sound asleep.

"I'm sorry I burned up your nice new rug," Darlene said soberly to Mrs. Thompson the next day, as she lay, bandaged like a mummy, in her bed at home.

"Oh, my dear child," cried Mrs. Thompson, tears in her pretty eyes. "What is a rug or a house or anything in the world compared to our loved ones? You'll never know what a dreadful shock it was when we returned home to find firemen and neighbors gathered about the part of our house left standing, but no sign of any children at all.

"Until you are grown, with a family of your own, you will never realize how grateful we are to you. If Evelyn had come, she and our children would surely have died in the fire, for she has always fallen asleep early in the evening, and has not awakened until our return. It was only because you awoke from your doze and heard Cookie's warning that your lives were spared. Faithful little dog, she's going to be all right, too, as soon as her paws are healed. And don't forget that both of you will have a suitable reward for your bravery.

"But we mustn't talk any more now. No one knows how the fire started, but our house was well insured and we can rebuild. The most important thing, however, is that everyone was saved and that you are going to be all right." She smiled tearfully up at mother.

"Yes, the doctor says that the burns, while painful, will heal over smoothly," mother answered. "I, too, am devoutly thankful that the lives of our dear ones were spared. And I am also very proud that my daughter remembered her responsibility toward those in her care. That is something that is to me the best reward of all!"

Darlene tried to smile, although the effort was a painful one. But smile she did as she said, "Well, all I can say is this: I don't think that any other baby sitter I ever heard about had as much excitement as I did on my very first night. I hope that my next baby-sitting job is a little more quiet and peaceful!"

13
Roundup from the Sky

I'D CERTAINLY like to see a real cowboy while I'm visiting over here at Grandma Grace's," said Marilyn. She stretched out on the green lawn and began to look for four-leaf clovers.

"So would I! And maybe I could ride on his horse. Wouldn't that be fun?" added seven-year-old Stephen Joel. His brown eyes sparkled at the thought of riding a prancing pony down the main street of Burns.

"What does a cowboy look like, anyway?" he questioned his sister.

"Oh, he's a man who wears a silk shirt with a bright bandanna neckerchief and big woolly chaps and a big hat and—oh, yes—high-heeled cowboy boots with pointed toes and silver spurs that jangle when he walks."

"Ho!" sneered Cedric. "Isn't that just like a girl? What a foolish idea! A cowboy doesn't look like that at all."

"He does too," stoutly maintained Marilyn. "I know

135

he does, because I've seen magazine pictures of cowboys, and they were dressed exactly that way."

"Maybe you've seen such photographs, Miss Smarty, but those weren't real buckaroos. Those were just dude ranch folks all dressed up to impress their city guests. Real cowboys out here on the range ride hard and work long hours. And they wear plain shirts, with tight-fitting, belted overalls, and old weatherbeaten hats. They *do* wear high-heeled boots, but only because that kind fit best into the stirrups—not for looks."

Marilyn and Stephen looked so crestfallen that Grandpa Jim got up out of his porch rocker and joined the quarreling children.

"Here, here," he smiled. "Let's settle the argument in a friendly way. Cedric's right about the buckaroo and his horse, youngsters, but even at that he hasn't described the very latest style in cowboy travel. Your grandmother and I are going out on the Bend Highway on an errand. Do you want to go with us and meet a modern cowboy?"

Grandpa and Grandma Lampshire laughed heartily at the speed with which their grandchildren clambered into the back of the Chevrolet pick-up truck.

"Hold on tight!" Grandpa called, "and don't lean out over the sides. Here we go."

A few blocks beyond the outskirts of the town he turned the truck off the highway and toward a small, tree-shaded house that sat companionably near a large building.

"I wonder why we're stopping here?" Marilyn asked the boys. "I don't see any horses out in the fields near by."

Cedric shrugged his shoulders, and Stephen's happy face clouded over with disappointment.

"Where's that cowboy we're going to see, Grandpa Jim? And where's his horse?" he asked, as his grandfather opened the cab door.

"Jump out, all of you," smiled Grandpa Jim. "Come along with us and you'll soon find out."

As they followed the Lampshires up the path, Stephen whispered to Marilyn.

"Maybe he keeps all his horses shut up in that big shed right over there. I imagine that's where all of them are. Don't you think so?"

But just then a sweet-faced young woman greeted them at the door, and in the midst of all the introductions Marilyn's answer was lost.

"So these are your young visitors for the summer," Mrs. Roe Davis said, as she smiled at the children. "Come right in. My daughters, Lola and Mildred, will be especially glad to meet you, for some years ago they studied piano from your mother, when she taught school over here.

"You arrived at the right time, for they and their father have just come in from a morning ride down to the White Horse Ranch. Roe had to go there to locate a band of horses, and urged all of us to ride with him. However, I couldn't spare the time from needed household tasks. Yesterday we rode down to Cottage Grove, and tomorrow we're going to Boise, Idaho."

White Horse Ranch—Cottage Grove, Oregon—Boise, Idaho—Cedric's head began to spin as he mentally calculated the distance of each trip. That historic old stage-coach stop, the White Horse Ranch in the south end of Harney County, was many hours' journey by car from Burns, as were the two cities.

"Then you'll have ridden hundreds of miles in less than three days!" he puzzled. "I don't see how you could do it and still be back here this early, even with a new car."

"New car!" interrupted Marilyn. "Why, he doesn't even use a car. Does he, Mrs. Davis? He must be the cowboy that Grandpa Jim told us we were coming to see, and so I'm sure he'd ride horseback. But I—well, I don't understand how any horses could go that far in two or three days."

"Well, well, so you're wondering about my horses," laughed Mr. Davis good-naturedly. He shook hands with everyone and then sat down with Stephen on his knee. "Would you like to see what carries me so swiftly over the country?"

Stephen nodded his head and smiled shyly up at the friendly speaker.

"Is he white? I guess he must be, if you got him at the White Horse Ranch when you went down to look at those horses. Could I see him now, please?"

"Of course you may. Come along, all of you."

Stephen and Marilyn clasped hands tightly as they skipped along to the large building.

"Just think! Now we're really going to see what they look like," whispered the little boy to his sister. "And I'm going to ask if I can ride on that white pony. Maybe he'll let me. He seems awfully nice."

But the children's wide eyes saw no horses of any

kind in that large building. For when Mr. Davis opened the doors, they saw, instead of horses, several shiny airplanes.

"Oh, oh!" exclaimed Cedric, grinning sheepishly. "I understand now. I should have known what you meant when you talked about traveling so far in such a short time. But Grandpa Jim kept talking about a modern cowboy, you see, and naturally I didn't even think about airplanes."

"But—but I want to see a horse," burst forth Stephen, his mouth drooping. "I've seen lots of airplanes."

"Well, perhaps you've seen many planes, but you've never seen anyone use a plane as Roe Davis does," said Grandma Grace. "Perhaps he'll tell you about his work while I talk to Mrs. Davis for a few minutes."

"Oh, please do tell us," begged Marilyn, as they returned to the house and sat down. "I'd certainly like to know how you can be called a cowboy when you don't even ride horseback."

"Well, it's quite a long story," smiled Mr. Davis, "but I'll try to give you the main facts, partly as outlined in *Newsweek* magazine and partly as I can recall other experiences of interest to you.

"Some writers have called me a 'modern cowhand,' a sort of flying handyman who helps the many ranchers in the high desert country of southeastern Oregon. I've done several things, from sowing seed for the farmers and hunting coyotes with plane and shotgun, to rounding up herds of wild horses.

"About three years ago my partner, Bill Stevens, and I began hunting coyotes in my Piper Cub. We first began

working for some sheepmen, who hired us by the hour. Later on, the price of coyote pelts rose to fifteen dollars apiece, and in 1943 we bagged more than four hundred pelts. By the time prices had dropped we still had employment of the same type, for the Oregon Game Commission hired three teams of pilots and gunners to destroy these prairie wolves which prey upon cattle and game. In February, which is the mating season, Bill and I bagged 137 coyotes in fifty-seven hours.

"I was the pilot, and Bill was the gunner, using a shotgun loaded with BB shot. We found that coyote hunting by air was the most successful over the sagebrush range at a height of about five hundred feet. At that height the tracks of rabbits, deer, and coyotes can best be seen in the snow."

"Can you really see the coyote plainly, Mr. Davis?" breathlessly asked Marilyn.

"Indeed we can," nodded the cowboy-pilot. "Coyotes run about twenty-five miles an hour and usually travel in pairs or families. They run in packs from the last of December to the first part of February, which, as I have already told you, is the coyote mating season.

"Sometimes we have seen as many as eleven coyotes in a pack. We watch, and try to locate them at their dens in the sagebrush up the little ravines. They often choose a shallow badger hole from three to six feet back in the top of a little hill, because they don't care much about digging out the dens themselves.

"We fly about 150 feet above the ground to locate the coyote. When we see him we come down to a distance of only twenty feet above the ground, as when pelt hunting we hunt mostly in open country where we can land for a pickup, and take off again."

"You mean you save the animal's fur?" cried Stephen. "How can you stop to pick up the coyote?"

"Indeed we save the pelt," smiled the pilot. "If we're on wheels, we land about a quarter of a mile away, or, if the landing place is not suitable, we just let the prairie wolf run until we can shoot and then land. But when the snow is good, we fly on skis. Here is a picture showing the plane on skis and three of the coyotes killed at that time."

"Does your gunner always kill the animals? Or do any of the wounded ones try to attack you?" breathlessly questioned Cedric.

"Bill's a mighty good shot, missing only about one in every five shots," answered Mr. Davis. "He has to shoot from the left side of the plane, too, with time for only one shot. If this misses, the plane has to take a long sweep and come back for a second run. Whenever he sees a pair he tries to kill the male first, for the female will stay beside the body of her mate. But if the female is killed first, the male tries to run away.

"And, by the way, I heard an interesting fact as to how the male coyote cares for the young ones if the female is killed. I can't verify this statement but I was told that the male will go out to hunt, will eat the food, and will then from his stomach return this predigested food for the pups. At the age of seven weeks the pups are able to eat solid food.

"But to get back to your question, Cedric," he continued, "I can say that I've had a few exciting experiences in which a wounded animal tried to attack me. One old fellow became pretty wise after escaping two plane runs. We had quite a time when he began dodging us instead of running straight ahead. But at last Bill shot him, wounding him. After we had landed on skis, I began to follow the trail, and came suddenly upon the animal. Instead of being afraid, he started savagely toward me, and I had to shoot him with my pistol. At another time we saw an enraged coyote actually turn at bay and try to attack the airplane as we passed over him. Lola, will you please hand us that picture taken by Mr. Meyers? It's really a very unusual photograph." The children, their heads together, gazed at the picture.

"Ugh!" cried Marilyn. "It seems cruel to kill the poor things. I should think you'd hate to."

"No, you wouldn't, Marilyn, if you could see how savage these creatures become," Mr. Davis continued soberly. "They show no pity for harmless animals, and will kill young deer and antelope, as well as calves and lambs.

"At one time I watched two coyotes stalking two deer: a doe and her tiny fawn. One wily old coyote kept the brave mother deer busy by repeatedly rushing at her from the front while the second coyote sneaked in behind to try to kill the helpless little fawn. Both of the beasts were big fellows, and even in ten inches of snow they could have kept up these tactics until the mother deer was completely exhausted. Then they planned to rush in and hamstring the deer—cut the muscles in her hind legs so that her legs would give way. After that she would be unable to defend herself or her fawn. We didn't wait for this to happen. We shot those two coyotes right then and there.

"I've seen them try the same tactics in spring lambing time, stalking an old ewe with her lamb snuggled right up against her. Coyotes are more destructive at this time of year than at any other, because the lambs and calves are small then and unable to defend themselves.

"These prairie wolves also rob the nests of ducks and geese, and eat the young ones. After the lake freezes over, they will paw open muskrat houses that stick up out of the ice. In fact, a woman at one of the bird refuge headquarters called me one day to come by plane and shoot a sly old coyote who sneaked into her barnyard every morning and carried away a fat chicken for his breakfast."

"I still can't see how you can bring home all those coyotes in that little plane," interrupted Marilyn, with a puzzled frown. "I wouldn't think you'd have room for all of them."

"That's a good question, Dad," laughed Lola. "You forgot to tell the children how you do that."

"In the wintertime we can land on skis and skin a coyote in four or five minutes," replied Mr. Davis. "To do this, we cut down the hind legs, skin the hind legs and tail, and then pull off his hide. Thus at night we would come in with from eight to eighteen or nineteen hides. The biggest catch we had was twenty-two coyotes in one day.

"The next procedure is to stretch the hides on boards —just as fox pelts are treated—one night turning the pelts with the fur in, and the next night turning the pelts with the fur out. Sometimes it is necessary to do some scraping for fat, but not often. Then the pelts dry for a week."

"I'm sorry to interrupt this conversation," said Grandpa Jim, "but it's time that we were on our way, for I have an appointment within half an hour. Yes, I know that you hate to leave, but perhaps Mr. Davis will tell you more about his hunting some other time."

"Oh, will you, please?" chorused the three interested listeners as they reluctantly rose to go.

"Of course, I'll be glad to," nodded Mr. Davis. "In fact, I was just getting nicely started. I hadn't even gotten as far as the large antelope herds we see, or the wild horses that we round up by plane, driving them up the hills into a little draw, where they are run down a chute into trucks. That also is an interesting story."

"Dad," broke in Mildred, "perhaps the youngsters would like several of these pictures to take along with them. Here's one that shows you in front of your airplane with 158 coyote hides—part of your winter's catch."

"We'd surely like to have them," replied Cedric. "And thank you so much for the story. I'd surely like to have a chance to see some of those wild horses you mentioned."

"Well, Cedric, I'll be busy for the next week or so, but perhaps sometime after that you can ride with me when I go down toward Catlow Valley. You'll see really wild horses down there, all right, and I'll show you how we round them up by plane.

"Wait a minute before you go," he added. "I have a present for each of you. I'll be right back."

"What do you suppose it can be?" Stephen whispered curiously to Marilyn.

"I can't imagine," she replied softly, shaking her head. "I expect it's another picture, though."

But Mr. Davis did not return with another picture. The youngsters gasped with delight when they saw the present that he handed to them, and each one said, "Oh, thank you, Mr. Davis," with heartfelt sincerity.

"I thought you'd like these soft coyote furs," he stated. "They make fine rugs for bedside use, and they'll last a long time. Now you'll remember my story each morning when you jump out of bed, for you'll step out on one of the coyotes that was rounded up by plane."

"Wasn't that fun, Stephen?" questioned Marilyn, as they drove away from the Davis home.

"It certainly was," agreed Stephen, clinging to the car with one hand and his precious coyote skin with the other. "We didn't see any horses, but this was even better, because I couldn't keep a horse in my bedroom, but I can keep a coyote rug by my bed."

"And am I lucky!" bragged Cedric. "Just think. Maybe I'm going to get to go with Mr. Davis in his Piper Cub. Won't Edwin wish he'd come over with us on our trip? Just wait till I go back and tell my big brother that I met a modern cowhand and rode with him over the eastern Oregon range on his roundup from the sky!"

14
Scarred for Life

O GWENDOLEN, we're going to have fun today. I only wish you could go on our seventh-grade picnic with us," June said excitedly.

She hastily wrapped the last nut-bread sandwich and squeezed it into the tin lunch pail on the very top of all the other delicious home-cooked food. She thought how good it would taste at noon; fat whole-wheat bread-and-jelly sandwiches, round orange-nut-bread sandwiches, plump black olives and tiny sweet pickles from papa's general merchandise store, and generous slices of sister Helen's rich chocolate cake.

"I wish I could too, but I can't. I'm only in the sixth grade. But I'll be here by the time you're home, so that you can tell me all about your trip," Gwendolen answered. "Do you think you'll get back by five o'clock, Juney?"

"I'm sure we will. Our teacher told us we'd try to return about four-thirty. She said she didn't want to be out too late with a big hayrack full of youngsters."

"No, and I don't blame her one bit either. I wouldn't want the responsibility of taking them in the first place," soberly added Mother Dalton. The surprised girls saw that her usually smiling face looked grave.

"Don't act so worried, Mamma," June spoke hastily. "Why, we've got a good driver, and his horses are as gentle as can be.

"Besides, we're only going three or four miles from town. We'll spend the day in Willow Grove and build a big bonfire on the riverbank so that we can toast marshmallows."

"Well, just the same, I can't help worrying," Mother Dalton continued. "I think this is the first class picnic to be held so far from Burns and the first wagon ride for such a large group. You'll be squeezed together like sardines."

"Well, if we are, some of us can be good little sardines. We'll sit along the sides of the wagon so that our legs can hang over the edge. That'll be more fun than crowding together in the middle anyway," June laughed.

"Now, June, listen to me," Mother Dalton warned. "You must promise me that whatever you do, you will not sit near the edge of the wagon. That is very dangerous. The horses might become frightened and run away. Or you might be caught on the side of the wagon and dragged along. I have known of several very serious accidents that happened in just such a manner."

"I'll be careful, Mamma. Really I will. After all, I'm not a baby any more. I can take care of myself!" June answered almost sharply, impatient to be on her way to the appointed meeting place.

Giving her mother a hasty kiss, June grabbed her broad-brimmed straw hat and tin lunch bucket, and hurried out the door after Gwendolen. It was not until the white picket gate had swung shut behind them that June spoke.

"Whew! I was afraid that mamma'd call me back and make me promise point blank not to sit on the side of the wagon. And that's exactly what some of us want to do. Frank said it's lots of fun. He said he'd ridden that way ever so many times on his uncle's hayrack."

"But isn't it really dangerous?" Gwendolen questioned anxiously. "It would be dreadful if anything went wrong and you got hurt. O Juney! I couldn't stand that." Tears sprang to her blue eyes as she looked at her friend.

June laughed gaily as she flung her arms around her chum and gave her a hug.

"Now, don't be a fraidy cat! Nothing's going to happen except things that are fun. And I'll be back this afternoon to tell you all about our seventh-grade picnic."

Gwendolen tried to look cheerful as she waved goodby, but her lips stopped smiling as soon as June rounded the corner on Main Street. She tried hard to feel that all would be well with the day's outing, but deep down inside she wished wholeheartedly that June had listened more closely to Mother Dalton.

But June was not at all worried. She hurried breathlessly on her way, quite unmindful of her mother's warning, intent only on the fun-filled hours ahead.

"Well, you're here at last. Now we can start," called Hazel. "We were beginning to wonder what had happened to you."

"Nothing happened," June sang out. "I just stopped to talk with Gwendolen for a few minutes. I'm all ready. Where's the wagon?"

"Listen and you'll hear the team coming now," Frank answered.

Amid choking dust swirls the big team of horses pulled the heavy wagon into view. With wild cries of joy the entire seventh-grade class clambered aboard and chose places for the gala ride.

"Please, boys and girls, when you sit down be careful to stay away from the edge of the wagon," the teacher warned. "Although the horses are very gentle, it is still possible that they could become frightened. Since I'm responsible for your safety today I want to be very sure that you run no risks."

All during the ride several of the boys grumbled that "there's always something to take the joy out of life." But June saw that they, as well as the rest of the class, carefully followed their teacher's advice and crowded together toward the center of the wagon bed.

June thought she had never had so much fun. The ride itself was thrilling, with the horse-drawn wagon lumbering along over the rutted road, past the tree-shaded Silvies River, up the steep gray sagebrush hills, and down into the green meadows of Willow Grove.

The picnickers agreed that their camp treat of marshmallows toasted golden brown over the campfire's red coals was surely a perfect dessert for a delicious noon meal. One and all moaned that they were simply too stuffed to play any more games. But soon they began to run wildly here and there in the willow clumps, playing blindman's buff, black man, and run, sheep, run.

"Oh! I hate to leave," sighed June as she and Frances and Hazel gathered up their lunch pails and climbed wearily into the waiting wagon. "Hasn't it been fun?"

"It certainly has," Hazel groaned, "but I'm so stiff and sore from running that I can hardly move. My! but we'll all be tired tomorrow!"

"Well, we don't have to go to school until afternoon to get our report cards," Frances said cheerily. "So we can all sleep late in the morning."

"Yes, and I'm certainly going to," agreed June. "Gwendolen's going to stay all night at my house, and we'll probably talk so long about the picnic that we won't wake up very early in the morning.

"But say, girls, I expect I will get up fairly early, after all. I almost forgot that papa told me to come over to the store by nine o'clock. He wants me to look at some catalog pictures of high-laced hiking boots. He's half-promised me a pair for my thirteenth birthday, June 1. And how I hope I get them to wear on our Campfire girls camping trip!"

"All aboard, everybody. We're late now," called out their smiling classmate, Harley, who had won permission to drive part of the way home. "Hurry up. Here we go."

Quickly the girls took the same places they had occupied on the morning ride. With increasing weariness they watched as the lengthening shadows forecast the fast-falling eastern Oregon dusk.

"I'm so tired I can't stand up a minute longer. I'm going to sit down," June said.

"Where?" inquired Hazel. "All the places in the middle of the wagon are taken."

"Then I'll sit down right here," June replied. "Why can't we sit cross-legged and lean back against each other? That wouldn't be quite so tiresome as standing up for another two miles."

"Well, we can try, but it doesn't look as though there'd be much room," Hazel answered doubtfully.

June soon learned that Hazel was right. For squirm and turn as they could, they found no place for their knees without poking them into their classmates' backs.

"I'm going to turn around and let my legs dangle outside," June finally announced in disgust. "I'll have to stand up if I don't, and I'm simply too tired to do that."

"All right! Then I will too," Hazel agreed, and soon whispers of "Me too" were heard, as weary picnickers stretched their cramped legs over the wagon's edge and let them dangle limply.

"Better be careful, or teacher'll see us!" warned Frank in a low voice. "You know she said not to do this, and the driver'd make us stop in a minute."

"Oh, teacher's too tired even to turn around to look at us. And the driver's so busy watching Harley that he's not paying any attention either," June scoffed. "Anyway, what in the world could possibly happen to us out here on this country road? There isn't a thing that could hurt us. It'll be all——"

June felt the words jerked right out of her mouth as the frightened horses shied at a coiled rattlesnake, and the heavy wagon lurched toward the side of the lane.

"Hang on! Hang on tight," she heard the driver yell frantically. As he grabbed the reins she saw that he and Harley were both pulling with all their might against the plunging, rearing horses.

"Whoa there! Whoa!" she heard him shout above the children's frightened screams as they hastily scrambled away from the wagon's edge and toward the center safety zone.

As June tried desperately to loosen herself from her wedged-in position she felt the wagon slide sickeningly off the dirt road. Her terrified eyes stared in unbelieving horror as it swung in a deadly arc. Closer, ever closer it came to the cruel barbed-wire fence that at this exact spot ran close beside the country lane.

Frantically she pushed against the wooden sideboards. But even as her muscles strained with the effort, she knew despairingly that it was no use—no use at all. She saw that she was trapped—trapped as in a vise—with the tearing wire barbs coming nearer and nearer.

And then June felt a dreadful tearing, searing agony across her legs. "Help!" she screamed. "Help! I'm caught in the barbed wire." But her voice was lost in the shouts and yells of the frightened seventh-grade pupils, whose eyes were turned toward the straining horses.

One! Two! Three! June felt herself dragged along the wire and against three fence posts. Then great waves of pain swept over her and drowned the liquid fire in her bleeding legs.

June never knew when the white-faced drivers pulled the lathered horses to a full stop. From a great distance she heard the hushed voices of her classmates and teacher as they gently lifted her up onto the wagon and bent over the terrible gaping wounds almost encircling her legs. Fragments of their tearful conversation swirled dizzily through her head. She thought how strange it was to hear them speak so pityingly of someone named June Dalton.

"We must get her to a doctor at once!"

"Poor child! I'm afraid she'll never walk again."

"She'll be in bed for months and months. Oh, it's dreadful!"

"Shouldn't we do something to stop the bleeding? Look! The barbed wire caught her right below the knees."

Just as the wagon started on its swift jolting ride to Burns, June gritted her teeth and rolled over onto her stomach. Dimly she realized that if she must spend months in bed she could not permit her back to be bruised from the wagon's jolting. She could never quite remember that terrible ride or how long it took to reach her white-faced mother and the sober-faced doctors who stood beside her hastily moved bed in the big front parlor.

She knew only that before she floated into complete unconsciousness she must speak to them. She must tell Mother Dalton how sorry she was to have ruined the crisp new gingham school dress and the long black cotton stockings, now torn to shreds. Vaguely she remembered hearing that one should never eat a meal before taking an anesthetic. Her thick tongue struggled to warn them.

"I—I ate——" she gasped.

"Now, now, June. Just lie still," warned kind Dr. Griffith while Dr. Saurman carefully adjusted the chloroform mask. "Don't try to talk."

"Marshmallows! I ate 'em!" June's voice croaked triumphantly, and then she felt herself shooting out into a whirling boundless space full of shining stars.

June never knew when a sobbing Gwendolen was turned away from her door that evening. Nor did she hear the tearful voices of Father and Mother Dalton after their talk with the doctors.

"I can't bear it, Mamma," wept Mr. Dalton. "Just think! Our girl was going to have her hiking boots for a birthday present. She wanted those more than anything in the world. But what good will boots do her if the doctors have to amputate one leg!"

"They can't, Jim. We can't let them do it today. I know they're good doctors and they've done all they can, but still she's burning up with fever. I'm going to ask them to wait until tomorrow to decide.

"Tomorrow all the school children of every church are meeting together for prayer for June's recovery. They themselves have asked the ministers to arrange for this special service. Surely their faith will be rewarded. We *must* wait!"

Long weeks afterward, when June was safely out of the "Valley of the Shadow" she heard the story of the churches' special services, when the prayers of all the school children and their parents ascended in her behalf. June felt the tears streaking down her pale cheeks as she listened. But they were happy tears, for by now she knew that she would walk again and that she would be able to wear the beautiful new boots that papa had placed so proudly on the table near her bed.

June felt that she could never repay everyone for all that they had done. She thought of the faithful doctors, her kind mother and father, her older sisters and brothers, the school friends who so faithfully visited her, and little sister Mildred, who cheerfully gave up her tomboyish out-of-doors fun to stay indoors all that beautiful summer and play games and "paper dolls" with the invalid.

She knew that she would never forget any of these friends. But she was especially grateful to the Byrd sisters —Evelyn, Marjorie, and Gladys—who played the violin and piano, and sang like real songbirds; to Laura Thornburg, who made countless trips to the library for good books, and to thoughtful Mrs. Lampshire, who almost daily brought delicious tray surprises of specially prepared food from her home next door.

But when her entire seventh-grade class came for a very quiet belated surprise birthday party, June felt that she could wish for nothing more.

"It's wonderful to have such good friends and to know that soon I'll be able to be up on crutches," she said that evening to Gwendolen, who had run over for her usual after-supper visit. "I can hardly realize even yet that I'm really going to be all right."

She flinched as Gwendolen leaned over and gently touched the deep red scars that almost encircled June's legs.

"Will they always show, June?" she asked sorrowfully.

"Yes, those scars will always show. And for a long time they'll be more or less painful, the doctors said. But I'm so thankful to have my legs that I wouldn't dare complain. It makes me shudder to think how near I came to losing them.

"You know, Gwendolen, you were right that day of the picnic when you felt that something was going to happen to me. Oh, I don't mean that you could look into the future, but you knew how rude I was to mamma when she warned me to be careful. You didn't have to think very hard to know that an accident might happen."

"I guess things always go wrong when we disobey our parents," Gwendolen soberly remarked.

"Well, I've learned my lesson the hard way," June added. "Believe me, from now on whenever I think of going against mother's wishes I'll just look down at these awful scars. They'll be warning enough for me. I'll never disobey again."